Disney · PIXAR

INSIDE OUT 2

Published by Scholastic Australia in 2024.

Scholastic Australia Pty Limited
PO Box 579 Gosford NSW 2250
ABN 11 000 614 577
www.scholastic.com.au

Part of the Scholastic Group
Sydney • Auckland • New York • Toronto • London • Mexico City
New Delhi • Hong Kong • Buenos Aires • Puerto Rico

Design by Winnie Ho
Composition and layout by Susan Gerber

NATIONAL LIBRARY OF AUSTRALIA
A catalogue record for this book is available from the National Library of Australia

ISBN 978-1-76152-235-2

FSC www.fsc.org MIX Paper | Supporting responsible forestry FSC® C001695

Printed and bound in Australia by the Opus Group

This product is made of material from well-managed FSC®-certified forests, recycled materials, and other controlled sources.

DISNEY · PIXAR

INSIDE OUT 2

ALL IN THE MIND

By Meredith Rusu

SCHOLASTIC
SYDNEY AUCKLAND NEW YORK TORONTO LONDON MEXICO CITY
NEW DELHI HONG KONG BUENOS AIRES PUERTO RICO

MBARRASSMENT·ENNUI·ENVY·FEAR·JOY·SADNESS·ANGER·ANXIETY·DISG
NESS·ANGER·ANXIETY·DISGUST·EMBARRASSMENT·ENNUI·ENVY·FEAR·JOY
MBARRASSMENT·ENNUI·ENVY·FEAR·JOY·SADNESS·ANGER·ANXIETY·DISGU
EAR·JOY·SADNESS·ANGER·ANXIETY·DISGUST·EMBARRASSMENT·ENNUI·E
NVY·FEAR·JOY·SADNESS·ANGER·ANXIETY·DISGUST·EMBARRASSMENT·EN
NXIETY·DISGUST·EMBARRASSMENT·ENNUI·ENVY·FEAR·JOY·SADNESS·ANG
MENT·ENNUI·ENVY·FEAR·JOY·SADNESS·ANXIETY·DISGUST·EMBARRASSME
ETY·DISGUST·EMBARRASSMENT·ENNUI·ENVY·FEAR·JOY·SADNESS·ANGER
ENT·ENNUI·ENVY·FEAR·JOY·SADNESS·ANGER·ANXIETY·DISGUST·EMBARR
·ANGER·ANXIETY·DISGUST·EMBARRASSMENT·ENNUI·ENVY·FEAR·JOY·SAD
ASSMENT·ENNUI·ENVY·FEAR·JOY·SADNESS·ANXIETY·DISGUST·EMBARRAS
SADNESS·ANGER·ANXIETY·DISGUST·EMBARRASSMENT·ENNUI·ENVY·FEAR·
MBARRASSMENT·ENNUI·ENVY·FEAR·JOY·SADNESS·ANGER·ANXIETY·DISG
NESS·ANGER·ANXIETY·DISGUST·EMBARRASSMENT·ENNUI·ENVY·FEAR·JOY
MBARRASSMENT·ENNUI·ENVY·FEAR·JOY·SADNESS·ANGER·ANXIETY·DISGU
EAR·JOY·SADNESS·ANGER·ANXIETY·DISGUST·EMBARRASSMENT·ENNUI·E
NVY·FEAR·JOY·SADNESS·ANGER·ANXIETY·DISGUST·EMBARRASSMENT·EN
NXIETY·DISGUST·EMBARRASSMENT·ENNUI·ENVY·FEAR·JOY·SADNESS·ANG
MENT·ENNUI·ENVY·FEAR·JOY·SADNESS·ANXIETY·DISGUST·EMBARRASSME
ETY·DISGUST·EMBARRASSMENT·ENNUI·ENVY·FEAR·JOY·SADNESS·ANGER·
ENT·ENNUI·ENVY·FEAR·JOY·SADNESS·ANGER·ANXIETY·DISGUST·EMBARR
·ANGER·ANXIETY·DISGUST·EMBARRASSMENT·ENNUI·ENVY·FEAR·JOY·SAD
ASSMENT·ENNUI·ENVY·FEAR·JOY·SADNESS·ANXIETY·DISGUST·EMBARRA
SADNESS·ANGER·ANXIETY·DISGUST·EMBARRASSMENT·ENNUI·ENVY·FEAR·
MBARRASSMENT·ENNUI·ENVY·FEAR·JOY·SADNESS·ANGER·ANXIETY·DISG
NESS·ANGER·ANXIETY·DISGUST·EMBARRASSMENT·ENNUI·ENVY·FEAR·JO
MBARRASSMENT·ENNUI·ENVY·FEAR·JOY·SADNESS·ANGER·ANXIETY·DISG
EAR·JOY·SADNESS·ANGER·ANXIETY·DISGUST·EMBARRASSMENT·ENNUI·E
NVY·FEAR·JOY·SADNESS·ANGER·ANXIETY·DISGUST·EMBARRASSMENT·EN
XIETY·DISGUST·EMBARRASSMENT·ENNUI·ENVY·FEAR·JOY·SADNESS·ANG
MENT·ENNUI·ENVY·FEAR·JOY·SADNESS·ANXIETY·DISGUST·EMBARRASSME
ETY·DISGUST·EMBARRASSMENT·ENNUI·ENVY·FEAR·JOY·SADNESS·ANGER·
ENT·ENNUI·ENVY·FEAR·JOY·SADNESS·ANGER·ANXIETY·DISGUST·EMBARR
·ANGER·ANXIETY·DISGUST·EMBARRASSMENT·ENNUI·ENVY·FEAR·JOY·SAD
ASSMENT·ENNUI·ENVY·FEAR·JOY·SADNESS·ANXIETY·DISGUST·EMBARRA

Chapter 1

"Whoa!"

Twelve-year-old Riley leapt out of the way of a tall student just in time. He'd nearly crashed into her. Riley's backpack slipped from her arm, spilling papers, pencils, and eraser tops onto the floor. Her hockey puck keychain fell off its chain (for the hundredth time) and rolled along the hall.

"Sorry, kid!" the student shouted back before zipping around a corner.

Riley pulled a face. He could have helped her. She began stuffing her spilled school supplies into her backpack. The polished concrete floors of her middle school still looked strange to her: cold and harsh and weirdly institutional. The floors at her old school in Minnesota had been tile; she remembered that specifically because she'd always counted the number of tiles between each deep magenta runner proudly displaying the school mascot. (Go, Reindeer!)

But this wasn't her old school. Or Minnesota. This was fall in San Francisco, where she was still relatively new and no one really remembered her name yet, and there were so many kids that she couldn't even make her way through the hall without a near collision.

The familiar ache of homesickness welled up in her chest. Although Riley's life had slowly gotten easier over the past few months, this school and San Francisco still didn't feel like *home*. Would things ever feel normal again?

The warning bell rang. She was going to be late.

"Ahhh! What do we do? What do we do?"

Fear flailed his wobbly purple arms. Beside him, all Riley's other Emotions—Joy, Sadness, Anger, and Disgust—watched a screen showing Riley's perspective as she struggled to gather her stuff.

A console stretched before them. It was dotted with colorful buttons and levers that connected the Emotions to Riley. Smooth metal tracks looped around the room, carrying glowing spheres of various colors—mostly happy golden—which represented Riley's memories. The spheres whizzed and whirled into tubes that led to the depths of Riley's mind, fueling the beautiful Islands of Personality, which stood proud and tall beyond the grand windows of the command center.

This was Riley's Headquarters, fondly referred to as HQ by her Emotions, all of whom shared a common goal: to keep their girl safe and happy.

That was the *opposite* of what was happening right now.

"We're going to be late!" Fear cried. "The teacher will kick us out!"

"Riley's not going to get kicked out," Joy, glowing with golden self-assurance, told him. Joy prided herself on staying calm when things spun out of control. After all, there wasn't any sticky situation that couldn't be turned around with a positive spin. They just had to look on the bright side.

"Has this floor ever been *cleaned*?" Disgust said, dramatically brushing a green strand of hair from her face as Riley picked up a dusty, slightly chewed pencil. "Eww!" Disgust gagged. "This isn't even our pencil! Gross!" Riley chucked the pencil away.

"I know who I'd clean the floor with," Anger said, pounding a fist into his opposite palm. "That punk who knocked into us!"

"He didn't even see us," Sadness moaned. "No one ever sees us. It was never like this back in Minnesota."

Sadness instinctively touched a glowing white button on the console, turning it a watery blue. Riley shed a tear.

Joy gently grasped Sadness's hand. "I know she needs you," Joy said with a comforting smile. "But right now we need to help her get to class. There will be time to let her feel the sadness—at home, with Mom and Dad."

"Okay," Sadness agreed. She removed her hand, and the button turned white once more.

Joy couldn't help thinking that it still felt a little strange to be working in tandem with Sadness and allowing Riley's good and not-so-good feelings to flow freely. Not long before, Joy would have tried to stop Sadness from overtaking Riley's feelings and memories. But doing that had proven disastrous.

When Riley and her parents had first moved to San Francisco, everything had changed drastically and all at once. For all eleven years of her life, Riley had been a bubbly, goofy, and perpetually positive girl. Sure, she'd had her moments of frustration. But Mom and Dad liked to say that Riley was their spot of sunshine in the thickest of clouds—their sweet, silly little monkey.

But in San Francisco, Riley had turned sullen. Her best memories had faded from their normal golden glow to blue. And at first, Joy had thought that there was something wrong—that she, Joy, needed to work overtime to keep all Riley's memories glowing gold with happiness. She'd tried to stop Sadness from touching any of Riley's memories. In doing so, she had accidentally gotten both herself and Sadness swept away to the depths of Riley's mind. It had been a long, perilous journey to make it back to Headquarters.

Meanwhile, without Joy and Sadness in HQ, Riley hadn't acted like herself at all. She'd been extra nervous (thanks to Fear), extra moody (thanks to Disgust), and extra, *extra* angry (thanks to Anger). She'd even made the terrible decision to try to run away from home to go back to Minnesota. Luckily, Joy and Sadness had made it back to HQ just in time to stop her—but it had been up to Sadness to change Riley's mind.

Along their journey, Joy had realized that Riley needed to feel *all* her emotions—even sadness—to be her true self. With Sadness at the wheel, Riley was finally able to express how homesick she was to her parents so that they could help her feel better. And the help of others was one of the most powerful, positive forces in Riley's life.

Joy would never again make the mistake of holding back a fellow Emotion.

"We'll be able to let all the tears flow back at home," Joy assured Sadness. "Riley's even keeping a journal now. That will—"

"Is this yours?"

The Emotions jumped at the new voice. It was coming from what was on-screen.

Through Riley's eyes, they saw a girl standing in front of her, holding out the hockey puck keychain.

"Who is *that*?" asked Fear. "Why is she talking to us?"

"She's in some of our classes!" Disgust said. "I always thought her braids were so pretty. Why did our hair have to be stringy today?"

"What should we do?" Sadness asked uncertainly.

Riley accepted the keychain. "Yeah, thanks."

The girl bent down to help Riley pick up her stuff.

"Thanks for your help," said Riley.

"No problem!" the girl replied, handing Riley books and papers from the floor. "I'll see you in Mrs. Wilken's class. Good luck on the quiz today!"

"See you." Riley smiled as she watched the girl walk down the hall.

Later that night, the Emotions were settling in for some much-needed shut-eye. Sadness stretched and yawned as she snuggled under her soft blue bedspread. Anger adjusted his little nightcap. (Why didn't it ever seem big enough for his head?) Disgust and Fear, meanwhile, were already snoring away.

That was when . . .

"You guys, something incredible is happening!" Joy burst into the bedroom, her energy glowing as bright as the morning sunrise.

Fear jerked out of his slumber. "Red alert! Abandon ship!"

"Could you keep it down?" Disgust raised her sleep mask. "You do *not* want to see me if I don't get a full night's beauty sleep."

"Yeah, what are you so percolator peppy about?" Anger asked huffily. "It's after hours. Time to simmer things down, not boil them up."

"Okay, you guys are *not* going to believe this,"

Joy bubbled on. "I was doing some final checks before bed, and I found this platform on the floor I'd never seen before, and I thought, 'That's weird, why is this here? Where did it come from?' So I pushed a bunch of buttons—maybe I shouldn't have done that, but I had to see what would happen—and these doors popped up and . . . you guys just have to come and see!"

Yawning, the Emotions stumbled after Joy to a platform in HQ that now held a narrow cylinder with a set of doors.

"What is *that*?" Fear asked, suddenly nervous.

"It looks like an elevator," Disgust said.

"It is! And you'll never guess where it leads!" said Joy, bouncing with excitement.

"Do we—do we go down?" Sadness asked uncertainly.

"I am *not* getting in there," Fear said, trembling. "Nothing good comes from going down creepy elevators after ten p.m."

"But I already did!" said Joy. "It's totally safe and totally cool, I promise. Come on!"

Curious, Anger and Disgust stepped in first. The elevator descended and returned empty a few moments later. Fear hesitantly entered next.

Joy reached out to Sadness. "Sadness, you can squeeze in with Fear and me."

"I—I don't know if I should," Sadness said. "Something tells me . . . I don't know. I just don't want to mess anything up."

"You won't!" Joy insisted. "I promise!"

"No—you guys go first," Sadness said. "I'll stay here and keep an eye on things."

"Are you sure?" Joy asked, a little deflated.

Fear moved to leave. "Well, if Sadness isn't going, then I certainly don't have—"

But before he could finish, the doors closed, and instantly, the elevator plummeted through the depths of Riley's mind.

"I don't like this!" Fear clenched his eyes shut. "We shouldn't be riding this thing!"

"Just trust me!" Joy exclaimed. "You'll see!"

The ride lasted only moments, but to everyone except Joy, it felt like a roller coaster into the unknown. Finally, the elevator slowed to a halt, and the double doors whooshed open.

Fear's eyes grew wide. "What is this place?"

Before them stretched a cavernous hall with a babbling brook filled with what looked like memory spheres. Echoes of Riley's past adventures swirled in the stream. Up from the floor, glowing tendrils were growing like vines.

They stretched, reaching far above, toward the place where the Emotions had just come from—HQ.

Joy and Fear joined Disgust and Anger, who stood outside the elevator, too uncertain to move farther into the cavern. They stared in awe.

"What are those?" Disgust asked. "I've never seen anything *growing* in Riley's mind before."

"They must be something new!" Joy exclaimed. "I think they grow from her memories. See how there are memories in the water?" She stepped forward and reached out to touch one of the tendrils.

"Are you crazy?" Anger protested. "Don't touch that thing!"

"What if it bites you?" Fear urged.

"I've already touched it!" Joy insisted. "Listen!"

She gently strummed the string and it vibrated with a soothing hum.

I'm a good student, the string echoed in Riley's voice.

"Is that Riley?" asked Disgust.

"Why would she be talking down here?" Anger asked, confused.

"I don't know." Joy gazed up at the growing tendrils. "I think this is a deeper part of her. Something that's just forming. Maybe because she's twelve now."

She reached out to strum a few more delicate strings.

I'm smart.

I'm funny.

"What do they all mean?" Anger asked, confused.

"And where are they going?" Disgust looked up.

"You mean where are they *growing*?" Fear corrected her.

Joy's gaze never left the empty reaches above. "I guess we'll just have to wait and see."

Chapter 2

The next week, as Riley entered her social studies class, she noticed a lack of the usual pre-bell chatter. Everyone sat at their desks, reviewing note cards, chewing their nails, or staring off into space. And that meant one thing: presentation day.

"Woo! Presentation day!" Joy cheered.

"How can you be excited at a time like this?" cried Fear. "On the list of Most Terrifying Things, public speaking is definitely top three!"

"It'll be great!" Joy insisted. "Riley has been practicing for weeks." She recalled a memory of Riley rehearsing in her room and even in front of her parents. "She's got this in the bag."

The teacher had asked all the students to present an idea that they believed could change the world.

"I still think our presentation should have been about hockey," Anger grumbled.

"That's not even on topic," said Disgust. "How would *hockey* change the world?"

"It could change the world if more people watched it!" Anger argued. "They don't know what they're missing!"

Finally, class was underway, and the presentations began. The first presenter was a girl named Grace Hsieh. Her hands were shaking as she carried a large jar full of coins up to the front of the room. She stood behind a lectern and placed the jar on top.

"Hi, I'm Grace," she started with a tremble in her voice. "And this is my presentation on how the change in your couch could *change* the world." She picked up the jar by its lid. "Did you know—"

CRASH!

The jar fell to the ground, scattering coins around the classroom.

"Oh, no!" Grace cried. She dropped to the floor to pick up the coins. But in her haste, she bumped into the lectern, which knocked into the teacher's desk and tipped over a computer monitor . . . and then spilled a cup of coffee. The class erupted in laughter.

But there was one person who wasn't laughing: Riley.

"Oh, no," said Joy. "We should do something."

"No," said Disgust firmly. "Just back away. That girl is a social Titanic. Do not get on that ship!"

A tinkling sound suddenly echoed throughout Headquarters. The Emotions turned to see a pedestal rising from the floor. Bright wisps of light spiraled and intertwined together on top.

"Are those Riley's beliefs?" Disgust asked. "From her Belief System?"

That was what the Emotions had come to call the new space deep below Headquarters: the Belief System. The beautiful glowing strings grew from Riley's memories and echoed different things she believed in: *I'm great at hockey. I'm strong. I'm smart.* But the Emotions hadn't known exactly what the belief strings were growing toward until then.

"Are they forming *into* something?" Fear gasped.

"But why? What are they doing?" Sadness asked.

The light stabilized, revealing a perfectly twisted knot of belief strings. It looked like a radiant flower.

"Whoa," breathed Joy, in awe of the new addition to Headquarters. She approached the object and strummed it like a belief string.

I'm a good person, it said in Riley's voice.

At that moment, Riley got out of her seat and began picking up coins with Grace.

"It's okay," Riley whispered. "I drop things all the time. I'm Riley."

Another girl joined them.

Disgust gasped. "It's the girl from before! The one who helped us pick up our stuff!"

"Hello again," said the girl. "I'm Bree."

The three girls smiled at each other.

The bell rang, and Riley headed to her locker, relieved that that nightmare was finally over. After Grace's mishap, the other presentations moved along smoothly. Even Riley got through hers without too much drama. But she felt for Grace. She knew exactly what it was like to have a whole class staring and laughing at you. She wouldn't wish it on her worst enemy.

"Hey, Riley," said someone behind her.

Riley turned around. Grace and Bree were there.

"Thank you for your help earlier," said Grace. "I thought I was going to die up there all alone."

"Presentations should be illegal," said Riley. "Whoever thought those were a good idea?"

Grace giggled. Riley was happy to have cheered her up a little.

"I'm glad we ran into each other again," Bree said. "We should hang out sometime!"

"I'd love that!" Riley answered without hesitation. She knew she was being too enthusiastic, but this could be her chance to finally make some real friends at this school. She realized there was one complication.

"The only thing is that my hockey league is starting soon, so I'll have to work around practices and games and stuff. But I definitely want to hang out," Riley said.

Grace gasped. "Wait, you play hockey? *We* play hockey!"

"Seriously?" cried Riley. "That's amazing!"

"Which team are you playing for?" asked Bree.

"The Foghorns," replied Riley. "I played in Minnesota, so this will be my first team in San Francisco."

Grace's and Bree's jaws dropped.

"*We* play for the Foghorns!" exclaimed Grace, whipping out her phone to show Riley a team photo. "This is, like, fate. It's a little creepy, but I'm not mad about it."

Riley couldn't believe her luck. What were the odds of meeting two girls who played hockey *and* played for the same team as she did?

"Welcome to the team!" Bree cheered. "Now we can hang out all the time!"

"Definitely!" added Grace. "We'll introduce you to everyone during our next practice. How long have you been playing? What position are you? What was it like playing hockey in Minnesota? Am I asking too many questions?"

Riley laughed and closed her locker. As she walked side by side with her new friends, she thought, *Maybe this place could feel like home after all.*

Chapter 3

"Come on, Riley! You got this!"

Inside Headquarters, the Emotions were in a flurry as they watched Riley zoom toward the goal. It was the fall opener game for the Foghorns against the Polar Bears. And Riley wasn't just cleaning up on the ice—she was looking *good* doing it.

"She's going too fast!" Fear squeaked, covering his eyes. "She's going to crash into the wall!"

"Then the wall had better get out of our way." Anger cracked his knuckles. "Nothing's slowing down Riley today!"

"Are you even listening to yourself?" Disgust scoffed. "We are *not* face-planting against the wall."

"Of course we aren't." Joy mirrored Riley's skating expertise, gliding across HQ's floor in a fluid motion. "Because Riley is the best—"

BAM!

Fear shrieked. Riley had slammed into the wall! It wasn't a face-plant, but it was enough to knock her down to her butt on the ice.

"Ooooh," the Emotions all said, cringing. Butt ice wasn't a good look.

"How come the wall didn't get out of our way?" Disgust said, goading Anger.

"Don't . . . even . . ." Anger fumed. He hit a button on the console, sending a streak of red running across it.

Riley clenched her fist, upset with herself for not paying closer attention.

"Are you okay?" Bree, who was the Foghorns' goalie, shouted from across the ice. "Anything hurt?"

"Only my pride," Riley called back, recalling the phrase from a teen movie she'd seen recently.

Grace helped her up. "We've got a game to win. Let's do Thread the Needle!" she said eagerly. "I've been dying to try it!"

"Oh, no—not Thread the Needle!" Fear quavered. "It's not ready yet!"

Riley, Bree, and Grace had been inseparable for nearly a year both at school and at the ice rink. They had been practicing a new hockey maneuver in secret.

Joy smiled knowingly. "It's ready."

In a flash, Riley gained control of the puck from the opposing team. (*She's just* that *good!* Joy thought.) She passed it to Bree, who ricocheted it off the wall back to Riley, confusing their opponents. Riley looked across the ice at Grace, who was keeping pace with her near the left wall of the rink. Grace nodded and fell back.

"Do you think she can do it?" Sadness asked. "What if we miss?"

"We won't!" Joy insisted. She pressed a button on the console, and Riley shot forward toward the middle.

"Outta the way!" Anger pushed a lever. Riley careened between two players, narrowly missing them.

"Watch it!" Disgust chastised him. "We almost checked them."

"Fortune favors the brave," Anger retorted.

"Have you been reading Dad's motivational calendar again?" Disgust asked.

Anger arched an eyebrow. "Maybe."

Meanwhile, two opposing players were hot on Riley's trail. The taller of the two scowled and put on a burst of speed, shooting in front of Riley and blocking her shot toward the goal. The second opponent charged at Riley, trying to steal the puck.

"We're clear!" Joy exclaimed. "Ready . . . steady . . . now!"

Riley unexpectedly snapped the puck back through the second opponent's legs to Grace, who was waiting behind them—in the center of the ice, with a completely clear shot of the goal. Grace slapped the puck forward at lightning speed.

"Gooooooaallllll!" the Emotions cheered in Headquarters.

Riley's team formed a circle around her and Grace, cheering and hugging. Thread the Needle had worked! Not only that, but it had gotten them their first big win of the season.

"Joy, look at Riley's Sense of Self," Sadness whispered. "It's shining so bright."

Joy nodded. "That's our girl."

Ever since it appeared on Riley's presentation day, the Sense of Self had become Riley's guiding light, helping her make good choices. To Joy and the other Emotions, it was their masterpiece: a symbol of their hard work, patience, and endless love for Riley.

I'm a good person.

This single certainty, housed in a beautifully twisted knot of brilliant glowing strings, was what made Riley, well, Riley.

Joy took control of the console. "Oh, yeah, it's celebration time! And that means only one thing—the *Celly Dance*!"

Joy smashed down a flashing rainbow button on the console, and a disco ball lowered in Headquarters. Riley, Bree, and Grace began a wiggly, arm-flailing dance on the ice, complete with an imitation of a foghorn.

"Ahhh-woooga! Ahhh-woooga!" the three of them chanted together as the rest of the team laughed and clapped a thumping beat.

Joy still remembered when Riley, Bree, and Grace had come up with the Celly Dance. It had all started when they passed one of those inflatable arm-flailing guys at a car dealership as Riley's mom drove them to practice. The girls had taken turns mimicking its silly movements, and although no one could fully agree who had suggested it first, the Celly Dance became a staple of the Foghorns' victory celebrations.

"Oh, man, that dance gets me every time!" Joy cracked up.

"I like these friends," Sadness said.

"Me too," Joy said, wiping a happy tear from her eye. "Just look at how much Friendship Island has grown!"

The Emotions turned to gaze out at the Islands of

Personality beyond the windows. The core islands were still there, like always, although ever since Joy and Sadness's adventure, they had become intertwined, and they even sported a large Golden Gate Bridge connecting all of them. There was Family Island, featuring a statue of Riley's mom and dad with their arms circled around their daughter. And there was Hockey Island, complete with a Foghorns logo painted on a giant billboard. Honesty Island had its hall of justice high atop a mountain peak. And Joy's personal favorite, Goofball Island, was loaded with Ferris wheels and carnival games and a very weird-looking clown.

There were even a few smaller one-off islands that popped up and crumbled every now and then. In the past year alone, there had been several. Retro Island had appeared, then vanished. (Fanny packs had made a comeback *hard* at Bridgeview Middle School for about three months.) And then Royalty Island came and went just as quickly. (Thank goodness that had passed. Riley couldn't do a British accent to save her life.) Boy Band Island appeared and disappeared in a flash of pyro-technics, much to Disgust's relief.

But the island that had grown and expanded the

most was Friendship Island. It was bursting with framed snapshots of Riley's best times with Bree and Grace, all cascading like a waterfall of happy memories into a pool of stars and sparkles.

"It's like they're bringing out the best in Riley," Sadness said with a rare smile crossing her face.

"They sure are," said Joy.

Later that night, when HQ was darkened and Riley had long since fallen asleep, all the Emotions were snoring.

All except Joy.

She sat at the console, turning over in her hands the red memory sphere of Riley accidentally slamming into the ice rink wall. Riley had recalled it all afternoon long. Even in sleep, she was still thinking about it, because Dream Productions was sending up weird versions of the accident for Riley to dream about. In one dream, the wall crumbled with the impact. In another, Riley got ejected from the game for destroying the rink. Joy could feel Riley tossing and turning uneasily in her sleep.

Joy winced. *Of all the memories from today, why is Riley*

fixating on that one? she wondered. There had been so much to celebrate! The ice-butt moment was just a blip.

I wish these sorts of memories wouldn't weigh Riley down, Joy thought. *Everything is going so great. Riley's at her best when she remembers her best—not her worst.*

Now Dream Productions was sending up a warped image of a Zamboni crashing through the broken rink wall and chasing Riley on the ice, blasting a police siren.

"If only there was a tube that was a one-way ticket to the Back of the Mind," Joy mused, "where the bad memories that Riley doesn't need never got recalled . . ."

Joy furrowed her brow and looked down at the red memory sphere. She instinctively yanked on a cord, interrupting the feed from Dream Productions and turning the dream dark.

"Ever . . ." she said quietly.

She had an idea.

Chapter 4

The candles on the HQ screen twinkled. This was it—the biggest day of all days: Riley's birthday! And it was not just any birthday. Riley was . . .

"Turning thirteen!" Joy clasped the other Emotions in a massive hug. "Our girl is officially a teenager!"

"I know," Fear said, his mouth squished under Joy's embrace so that his words came out muffled. "Just think of all the new things to be afraid of."

"Aw," said Sadness, "it's Riley's last year of middle school. That's sad."

They watched Riley's birthday candles on-screen as she blew them out.

"Happy Birthday, monkey!" her mom and dad cheered. Then Riley's dad picked up a cake server to cut Riley the first piece.

"Ew," Disgust said, eyeing the monitor. "Did Dad think we wouldn't see him lick frosting off his finger?"

"You guys, stop focusing on the negative!" Joy spun around the room. "Our girl is growing up! There are so many incredible things to look forward to as a teenager. Like high school!"

"Let's just get through eighth grade first." Fear shuddered.

"And school dances!" Joy twirled.

"Does Riley know how to dance?" Fear quavered.

"And driving!" Joy cried.

"Driving?" Fear exclaimed. "Who said anything about driving?"

"Well, in a few years, anyway." Joy brushed Fear's worry aside. "But being a teenager is when the action happens! When Riley becomes her best self! Alongside her best friends!"

As if on cue, the doorbell rang at Riley's house. Bree and Grace, holding balloons and a box with a bow, were at the door.

"Ahhh!" screamed Riley.

"Ahhhhhh!" screamed Bree and Grace. "Happy birthday!"

"What's with all the screaming?" Anger asked. "Are we looking to start something?"

"The only thing that's starting is the party!" Joy slapped the rainbow button on the console, lowering the HQ disco ball.

Riley started the Celly Dance. *"Ahhh-woooga! Ahhh-woooga!"*

Bree and Grace joined in. Joy thought she might burst from happiness.

The girls bustled into the living room.

"Open your present!" Grace exclaimed.

The Emotions watched with curiosity as Riley tore open the gift.

"Oh my gosh!" Joy gasped. "Ohmygoshohmygoshoh-mygosh."

"I love it!" Riley squealed as she held up a colorful jacket inscribed with the signatures of her all-time favorite girl band, Get Up and Glow. "This is the limited-edition jacket! It's been sold out for months! How did you get it? How?"

"We have our ways," Bree said, winking at Grace.

"Bree means her dad works with a guy who knows a guy who—"

"Put it on!" Bree exclaimed. "Put it on!"

"Put it on!" Joy echoed in HQ.

Riley put the jacket on over her favorite T-shirt (which was getting a little too tight, even though Riley refused to admit it).

"It's *so* Glow Glamorous!" the girls all shrieked together.

Anger rubbed his temples. "Someone, please make it stop."

"I can't believe it," Joy said with her eyes shining. "Bree and Grace know Riley better than anyone. They love her so much."

Riley flung her arms around her friends. "You guys are the best! I love you so much!"

"We love you, too, Riley!" Bree and Grace smooshed their faces against Riley's cheeks.

Later that spring, the big event Riley thought would never get there finally arrived.

It wasn't middle school graduation. (That was the next week.)

It wasn't the Foghorns' hockey championship playoffs. (Those were the next month.)

And it wasn't getting her braces off. (That wouldn't be for a while. Riley had only just gotten them on.)

No, this event was bigger than all three of those combined.

Because that night, Riley, Bree, and Grace were attending their Very. First. Get Up and Glow concert.

Riley could scarcely tell if the vibrations in her chest were from the hum of the crowd or her own excited jitters. They were surrounded by a massive number of fans in a cavernous arena Riley knew well because it was where the professional hockey teams played their games during the season. The rink usually sported a freshly smoothed sheet of ice, and the stadium was normally so cold that your breath would form little puffs even in the nosebleed section. But that night, the floor was covered by a huge stage plastered with Get Up and Glow logos.

Grace's mom had gotten them tickets to see the band on tour as a middle school graduation gift—and now they were about to watch them perform in person.

"I can't believe we're here!" Riley couldn't stop smiling.

"Where's your mom's seat?" Bree asked Grace.

"Oh, she's somewhere up there." Grace pointed to the nosebleed section at the top of the arena. Her mom had generously given the girls better seats so they would have a great first-concert experience. "I think she's just as excited as we are."

"Your mom is so cool," Riley said.

"Speaking of cool, check this out." Grace took a huge slurp of her slushy and then stuck out her tongue. The center had been dyed neon blue by the frosty drink. "Lizard tongue!"

"Haha! Your tongue matches your nails!" Riley laughed, pointing to Grace's electric-blue nails.

"It's my new look!" Grace said, sticking out her tongue and wiggling her fingers. "Here—try some slushy! I swear, it makes your brain freeze blue!"

Riley took a huge gulp (from the opposite side of the cup Grace had been drinking from, because germs weirded her out). Then she immediately squeezed her eyes shut and shook her head. "Ack! Brain freeze!"

Just then, a huge roar went up from the crowd as the arena lights dimmed and several strobe lights began pulsing onstage.

"They're starting!" Bree shouted.

The three best friends jumped and screamed as the Get Up and Glow band members stepped into the spot-light. And as the first pounding beats of Riley's favorite song echoed throughout the arena, and as she fist-pumped and cheered in time along with Bree and Grace amid the sea of fans, Riley couldn't help thinking that for this one brief moment in time, she was right where she belonged.

Chapter 5

"This is Joy, coming to you live from inside Riley's mind!" Joy pretended to be an announcer. "And we're expecting a great championship today with the Foghorns!"

It was late June, exactly three weeks since middle school graduation. And now it was the final game of the hockey playoffs, against the Foghorns' rivals, the Sea Lions. Riley's team was in it to win it!

"Foghorns on three!" Riley was telling her team. "One, two, three, Foghorns!"

"Let me at 'em!" Anger cracked his knuckles and strode up to the console. With an expert smack of his fist, he pounded a glowing red "pump it up" button.

Riley powered past two opposing team members and slapped the puck into the goal.

"Goal!" Joy shouted. Riley's perspective shifted to

the stands, where her parents were dressed head to toe in white and teal to support her team.

"Go, Riley!" her mom and dad shouted.

Joy flushed with pride.

"Can you believe how strong and beautiful our girl is?" Joy asked the others. "Isn't she the best?"

"Sorry, what was that?" Fear looked up from his clipboard. "I was just finishing up the championship safety checklist. Gloves . . . kneepads . . . mouth guard—"

"No, no, no—not *that* mouth guard!" Disgust urgently hit a button on the console. Riley had almost picked up a teammate's mouth guard to put in *her* mouth!

Joy smiled and shook her head. Riley wouldn't be Riley without her team of Emotions there to support her. But right then, Joy was gosh-darned proud of their girl out there on the ice, leading *her* team to victory, with the love and support of her parents and friends.

"Oh, no, Joy. Look." Sadness interrupted Joy's thoughts and pointed to the screen.

The game was tied. Riley was just getting out of the penalty box for accidentally tripping another player. And there was only a minute left.

"How are we going to score in time?" Disgust asked.

"We need an idea!" Joy said, pulling a box of light bulbs from beneath the console.

Anger and Fear grabbed two different ideas and placed them in the console.

"We use our slap shot!" said Fear.

"We charge the goalie!" Anger asserted.

"But Grace hasn't scored yet!" Sadness noted.

Joy pulled out an idea and placed it in the console. "Riley's got this."

The Sense of Self glowed as Riley decided on the third idea. She smiled and nodded to Bree and Grace.

"C'mon, Riley," Joy whispered. Their girl was about to execute the play she'd perfected with her besties—the play they could do in their sleep because they worked so well together. Because that was what best friends did.

Bree ricocheted the puck off the wall to Riley.

Riley shot forward with a burst of speed. But three opponents were hot on her trail.

Ten seconds left. Nine . . . eight . . .

The goalie tensed, prepared to block the shot.

Riley's Sense of Self sparkled.

She snapped the puck back between the legs of the

opponent beside her. Grace was ready and waiting with a clear shot of the goal.

Three . . . two . . .

Grace took the shot.

"Goooooal!" cheered all the Emotions in HQ.

All Riley's teammates dogpiled her, Grace, and Bree on the ice. It was a collision of smiles and high fives and cheers of *"We won! We won the championship!"*

The entire team began the famous Celly Dance, and in HQ, Riley's Sense of Self cast a prismatic light that twinkled like diamonds.

The league president presented the championship trophy to the Foghorns. Riley, Grace, and Bree hoisted it in the air for their teammates to see.

"We did it!" Riley led them in a cheer. "Champions!"

Joy watched as a yellow memory sphere rolled into Headquarters. There was no better ending to a season—and an era! This was Riley, Bree, and Grace's final game on the Foghorns. High schoolers weren't allowed to play on the club team. With luck they'd all do well in the high school team tryouts that fall. But as for their time on the Foghorns, they had quite a victory to go out on.

As the team exited the ice, Grace hopped up on the

bench and raised her arms in triumph. "Funnel cake for all!" she yelled.

"Yeah!" everyone cheered.

"Aw, the postgame funnel cake tradition is my favorite," said Joy.

"I hope we still get to do this in high school," said Sadness.

"Of course!" Joy insisted. "Grace, Bree, and funnel cake aren't going anywhere!"

"Hey, girls!" someone suddenly called out behind Riley.

Riley and her friends turned to see a tall woman smiling at them. "Congratulations on your win!"

"That's the high school coach!" Joy gasped. And it wasn't just any high school coach. This was the *varsity* hockey coach, Coach Roberts. And she was congratulating *them* on their win!

Bree nudged Riley in the side. Her friends were as excited as she was.

"What a game!" Coach Roberts continued. "That last play, woo! The three of you were impressive."

"Thanks, Coach Roberts!" Riley said in a voice a little higher pitched than she intended.

"Look, it's last minute," the coach said, "but every year

I do a three-day skills camp. I invite all the best players in the area. It starts tomorrow. If you want, I'd love for you girls to come."

In Headquarters, the Emotions were as stunned as Riley was.

"Are we in a dream right now?" Fear said. "Please, can somebody pinch me?"

Anger punched him instead.

"Ow!" Fear exclaimed. "Definitely awake."

"If we impress Coach," Joy said, "she'll put the three of us on the team next year!"

"Oooh, the Fire Hawks!" Anger exclaimed as he put on a Fire Hawks cap. "Finally! A team I can get behind."

"What do you say?" Coach Roberts asked the girls.

Riley, Bree, and Grace answered in the affirmative.

"Yes!"

"Thank you so much!"

"We'll so be there!"

Coach Roberts nodded. "Great! We'll see ya tomorrow."

As she walked away, Riley huddled with her friends.

"Did that seriously just happen?" she asked. "Did the high school coach ask *us* to come to her skills camp?"

"This is big!" Bree agreed. "Bigger than big—wicked warped big!"

"We have to find our parents!" Grace exclaimed.

Together, the girls thundered up the bleachers to where their parents were talking.

"There are our champions!" Riley's mom exclaimed. "We were wondering where you were! We need some commemorative photographs!"

"For when our monkey is going to be a professional player someday!" Riley's dad said, scooping her up in a hug.

"Dad!" Riley laughed.

"You'll never believe what just happened!" Bree urgently told her mom and dad. "Coach Roberts just asked the three of us to go to her skills camp!"

"Coach Roberts?" Bree's dad gave her an odd look. "Wait—isn't that the other high school co—"

"That doesn't matter!" Bree said quickly. "Dad, she's a *varsity* coach. It's a huge deal for her to invite us. And the camp starts tomorrow!"

"Tomorrow?" Riley's mom asked, surprised.

"Tomorrow!" Riley's dad echoed. "That's great!"

"Is it?" Riley's mom gave him a pointed look. "That's kind of short notice."

"Can I go, Mom? Please?" Riley begged.

"I'm not sure . . ." Riley's mom said slowly. "Is this the overnight camp I've heard about? At the college campus?"

"Please, Mrs. Andersen, can Riley come with us?" Bree and Grace said.

"Hang on, girls," Bree's mom said. "We didn't say you could go yet, either."

"Pleeeeeease?" the three girls begged. "We can't say no to Coach Roberts!"

"Exactly! There's no saying no to the varsity coach!" Riley's dad insisted.

"You're not helping, honey." Riley's mom gave him an even more pointed look.

"Listen to Dad!" Anger shouted from HQ. "He gets us."

"Oh, no," Sadness said. "What do we do if Mom says no?"

For a gut-wrenching moment, Riley and the Emotions held their breath. But then Mom's face softened.

"Okay," Riley's mom said. "You three did just win the state championship. If anyone deserves to go, it's you."

"Oh, thank you!" Riley said. "Thank you, thank you, thank you!"

"Thank you!" Riley's dad squeezed her mom and jumped up and down.

"And us?" Bree and Grace turned hopefully to their parents.

Bree's mom and Grace's mom looked at each other, then at their husbands. "I guess we can't say no . . ."

"Ahhh!" Riley hugged her friends. "We're going to the skills camp!"

"Let's shove down some funnel cake and get packing!" Grace said with a fist pump.

The trio was starting to race off when suddenly Bree's and Grace's parents each put a hand on their daughters' shoulders.

"You all go ahead," Bree's dad said to Riley and her parents. "We'll be right there. We just need to talk with the girls for a sec."

"Oh, okay," Riley said.

"Are Grace and Bree in trouble?" asked Disgust. "They seem worried."

"Who could be worried at a time like this?" said Joy. "We just won the championship and now we're going to camp with our best friends!"

Dad put his arm around Riley's shoulders and started chanting, "Champions! Champions!" As Riley joined in, all worries faded from her mind.

Chapter 6

Later that night, Riley sat on her bed, taping her hockey stick in preparation for the hockey camp. She couldn't stop smiling. First they'd won the championship, and now she and her besties were invited to a skills camp—hosted by the varsity coach! Would it be hard? she wondered. Would she know anyone else there? Probably not, since it was mostly high schoolers. But she'd have Bree and Grace with her. Just wait until everyone saw what the three of them could do!

Her parents knocked on her half-open door.

"What a big day!" her mom said.

"Ha-ha! You're such an all-star!" Riley's dad picked her up in a huge hug and began rocking her back and forth. "You're going to knock that coach's skates off!"

"Dad, stop," Riley said, laughing. "It's just her hockey camp. Who knows what will happen?"

A sudden thought struck Riley: what if she *didn't* do well? What if she messed up so badly that Coach Roberts thought inviting Riley to the camp had been a mistake? The memory of getting a penalty for tripping another player during the championship game flashed through her mind.

"My penalty almost lost us the game today," Riley, downcast, told her parents. "What if I get to camp and screw it up?"

"Hey, don't talk like that," her dad said reassuringly. "You did great today, honey. Those Fire Hawks will be lucky to have you!"

"Yeah, I guess," Riley said, giving her dad a half smile.

"We're so proud of you." Riley's mom kissed the top of her head. That made her feel better.

"Night, monkey," said her dad.

Riley smiled, already feeling sleepy. "Night, Dad. Night, Mom."

"Oh, Riley's so hard on herself," said Sadness. Riley had fallen asleep, and the Emotions were discussing what had just happened. They hated seeing Riley happy one moment and then deflated by a painful memory the next.

Joy observed her fellow Emotions' expressions and took a deep breath. She hadn't been sure when she was going to be ready to show them the big idea she'd been working on. But now seemed like the perfect time.

"What if . . ." Joy started slowly, "what if we can make everything easier?"

"What do you mean, Joy?" asked Sadness.

"Behold!" Joy grabbed a long hook to open a panel in the ceiling. A tube was released, and it lowered to the floor. Joy had been adapting it—and secretly using it—for months. Anytime Riley had a memory roll through that made her feel less than her best self, Joy would send it straight to the back of Riley's mind, where it couldn't hurt her. "This is my super-high-tech Riley protection system!"

A piece of metal fell off the tube and clanged to the floor.

"Heh, heh." Joy scrambled to place it back on. "Don't look at that. It's fine."

"It's a high-tech-a-ma-whatsit?" Fear asked uncertainly.

"This is for all those memories that belong in the Back of the Mind!" Joy explained. She held up the blue memory sphere replaying Riley's penalty from the game. "Like this penalty one. It's weighing on her, so let's lighten the load!"

Joy placed the blue penalty sphere into the tube opening. She pulled back and released a plunger, springing the memory like a pinball up into the tube and out of sight. "This tube is a one-way expressway to 'we're not going to think about that right now'!"

Joy beamed as the other Emotions reacted, clearly impressed.

"Not bad, Joy." Anger nodded.

"You take such good care of Riley," Sadness concurred.

"Thanks." Joy mock polished her nails on her shoulder. "I try. Okay, let's do a sweep!"

The Emotions collected spheres from the memory wall that were negative, unfortunate, or just cringeworthy.

"Here's one where she waved at a guy who was actually waving at a girl behind her," said Disgust.

"Ohhh, that was so bad." Joy nodded. "Good choice."

"And here's when she forgot that girl's name," Anger said.

"That was super awkward," Joy agreed.

"What *was* her name?" Disgust asked.

Joy shrugged. "I don't know. Janet or something? Whatever, let's just get rid of it."

Together they loaded armfuls of unpleasant memories into Joy's jerry-rigged Back of the Mind tube. Joy closed the seal and pulled back on the plunger.

"We keep the best and toss the rest!" Joy proclaimed before shooting all the memory spheres to the depths of Riley's mind. Mission accomplished. What good were memories if they weren't the best ones to help their girl shine?

After one more quick sweep, the Emotions sent the remaining day's memories down to Long Term, then stretched and yawned.

"Good work, everybody," Joy said, selecting one final golden sphere from the memory wall. Inside played the memory of Riley, Bree, and Grace hoisting the championship trophy. She had special plans for that one. "You guys go get some shut-eye. Big day tomorrow. I'm just going to finish cleaning up a bit."

As Anger, Disgust, and Fear traipsed off to bed, Sadness lingered behind. "Joy?" she asked. "Are you taking that where I think you're taking that?"

Joy smiled. "You want to come this time?"

"Yes . . ." Sadness said hesitantly. "I mean, no. Oh, no, I really shouldn't."

Joy put an arm around Sadness's shoulders. "You know, you're the only one who hasn't been to the Belief System."

"Yeah," Sadness admitted. "It's just that it's new, and I know how important it is, and I don't want to mess it up or break it or burn it to the ground or anything."

"Sadness, you won't hurt it," Joy assured her. "I promise. Have I ever steered you wrong before?"

"Many times."

"Come on." Joy pressed a sequence of buttons on the platform to summon the elevator. "Where I go, you go." She held Sadness's hand as they stepped inside.

The depths of Riley's Belief System were unlike anything Sadness had ever seen before. She had heard the other Emotions talking about it for months. But seeing it for the first time took her breath away.

What stood before Joy and Sadness was a rich forest of glowing strings fed by a constant stream of memories from throughout Riley's mind.

"Whoa," Sadness breathed, her face bathed in the forest's glow.

"Pretty impressive, huh?" Joy beamed. She stepped forward and lightly strummed one of the strings.

Mom and Dad are proud of me.

Sadness timidly plucked a strand.

I'm kind.

"Aw, that's nice," Sadness said.

Joy and Sadness took turns strumming the different beliefs one by one.

Homework should be illegal. Get Up and Glow is the best band in the world. I'm a really good friend.

Then, gently, Joy placed the golden memory sphere of Riley's championship victory into the stream. A brilliant rainbow glow rippled throughout the water as the memory fed a new belief string that stretched up and attached itself to the rest of the system.

I'm a winner.

"Riley's the best," Sadness said, overwhelmed with love for their girl.

Joy nodded. "And it's only going to get better."

EMBARRASSMENT • ENNUI • ENVY • FEAR • JOY • SADNESS • ANGER • ANXIETY • DISGUST

Chapter 7

Beep. *Beep. Beep.*

Joy stirred in her sleep. Something was making a strange beeping sound. *Did Anger leave one of his burritos in the microwave again?* she wondered, half in a dream.

Beep. Beep. Beep.

She lifted her head groggily and listened. For a moment, the beeping stopped. *Hmmm.* Maybe she had imagined it? Joy rested her head back on her pillow.

Beep. Beep. Beep.

Now all the Emotions shot up in their beds, alarmed.

"What the heck is that?" Sadness asked.

They anxiously crept down the stairs from their bedroom and into central HQ. Anger held a bat just in case. The beeping was steady now and seemed to be coming from the console.

Joy walked over and scanned all the buttons. Everything looked normal—except for a tiny flashing red light.

Sadness leaned closer. "It's the Pooberty Alarm."

"Oh, yeah. I forgot about that thing," Joy said. The red button labeled PUBERTY ALARM had been a part of the console since the Mind Workers had modified it when Riley was twelve. So far, it hadn't done anything. The Emotions had figured it was there for decoration.

But now it blinked red and continued its incessant beeping.

Beep. Beep. Beep.

"What's it doing?" Fear asked nervously as they huddled closer.

BEEEEEEEEEEEEEEEP!

The Puberty Alarm blared a high-pitched siren.

"This is the end, people!" Fear freaked out. "It's the apocalypse!"

"Joy, make it stop!" Disgust plugged her ears with her fingers.

Joy frantically tried to smother the alarm with her hands, but it was no use. The siren was deafening. They had to get this thing out of HQ! Thinking fast, she wriggled the alarm loose and chucked it into her homemade Back of the Mind tube.

BEEEEeeeeeeeeep . . .

The siren faded and the Emotions breathed a sigh of relief.

"Whew. Problem solved," Joy said, feeling rather pleased with herself.

That was when . . .

CRASH!

The Emotions jumped and screamed once again. A massive wrecking ball had smashed into one of the windows in Headquarters! Shards of glass flew everywhere as the entire frame collapsed.

"What is going on?" Joy shouted.

They watched, horrified, as a construction lift rose outside the demolished window. It carried dozens of Mind Workers wearing hard hats and holding sledgehammers.

"Okay, let's clear it all out!" the foreman ordered, hopping down from the lift, with glass crunching under his steel-toed boots. "It's *demo day*!"

The Emotions gasped as Mind Workers poured into HQ. The Mind Workers cheerfully chatted even as they began demolishing walls and jackhammering the floor.

"What's going on? *Ahhh!*" Anger flared angrily—right next to a box of dynamite the Mind Workers had just set down.

"No, no, no!" Joy rushed over to settle him down before he blew Headquarters to smithereens.

Fear noticed the box of dynamite inches from Anger's flame and ran away screaming.

"Who *are* you people?" Disgust demanded as a worker smashed a hammer into the wall behind her. But the worker ignored her.

"Excuse me!" Joy ran to the foreman, who was holding a clipboard. "Are you in charge here? Could you do me a favor and *stop* tearing Headquarters apart?"

"No can do." The foreman clicked his pen. "Didn't ya hear? Permits just came through."

"Permits?" Joy asked, confused. "For what?"

The foreman dropped a stack of permits into Joy's hands. "Expanding the place! You know, for the others."

"Others? What others?" Joy cringed as something exploded across the room, billowing dust everywhere.

"They're not here yet?" the foreman asked. He put his pen in his pocket and called out, "Hey, Margie! You got that console?"

A Mind Worker opened a panel in the console and fiddled with some wiring. "Yup! She's all set!" She slammed the lid shut and locked it.

"Set with what?" Joy gripped her hair, distraught at the

chaos around her. What was happening to their beautiful Headquarters?

Suddenly, all the lights kicked on.

Riley was awake.

The foreman blew a whistle. "Lunch break!" he called to the workers.

"Wait—you can't leave it like this!" Joy wailed.

But it was no use. The workers filed out, crunching debris under their boots, just as the Emotions heard Riley's dad's voice on-screen.

"Come on, Riley! We're going to be late! Grace is waiting."

This wasn't good.

Riley groggily lifted her head off her pillow. She had a horrible taste in her mouth. It must have been from all that garlic pizza she'd celebrated with the night before. But worse than that, Riley simply felt . . . gross. Her face was oily. She ran a hand through her hair. *Ugh.* It was tangled and knotted. And her pajamas were sweaty, even though she'd kicked off the blankets in the middle of the night.

"Riley?" her mom asked, walking into the room. "Grace is waiting downstairs." She eyed Riley's empty suitcase and frowned. "You're not packed yet?"

"Ugh!" Riley shouted, inexplicably annoyed. *"You're always on me! Can't you lay off for, like, one second?"*

Her mom's eyes widened. "Riley, what's wrong?"

"Overreact much?" Disgust said, shooting Anger a look. Inside HQ, Anger had just pushed the button that had sent Riley into the tirade.

"I barely touched it!" Anger insisted. "Those morons broke the console!"

On-screen, Riley's mom was looking at her with concern. "Are you okay?"

"Oh, Mom looks sad." Sadness gently touched one of her watery blue buttons. Normally her pushing that button would make Riley sigh deeply. But not that day . . .

"I'm the worst!" Riley burst into tears.

Sadness held up her hands. "I barely touched it!"

"That's what I said!" Anger replied.

Disgust cracked her knuckles and approached the console. "Let the professional handle this."

Riley suddenly stopped crying and sniffed her armpit. *"I'm too gross to go to camp or anywhere ever again!"*

"Oh yeah, this thing is totally broken," Disgust agreed.

"But what do we do?" Fear panicked. "We can't help Riley without the controls!"

"Here, let's try this!" Joy rushed up with a long stick. "We'll tap the buttons from a distance."

On-screen, Riley's mom was talking. "You're not gross, honey. You're just changing. Remember that beautiful butterfly we saw in the park last week? It started as a caterpillar, and just like that caterpillar, you're about to get wings. Not literal wings . . ."

"What is she *talking* about?" Disgust asked as the whole group reached out with the stick from a distance.

"Easy," Joy cautioned them. "We'll just barely tap the button . . ."

The stick made contact.

"Oh my gosh, Mom! Just go away! Ugh!" Riley stormed out of the room.

The Emotions collapsed in a pile. Thanks to whatever those Mind Workers had done, it was going to be a long day.

Chapter 8

The Andersen family car rumbled along the road, and Riley and her Emotions soaked up the sights of their first visit to a college campus. San Francisco's busy city streets had fallen away a short while before, but here, on the wooded approach to the skills camp, it felt almost like a different world. Pathways meandered from the main road, leading up hills to modern academic buildings boasting wooden beams and entire walls of windows. A few summer college students, reading or listening to music, reclined on blankets stretched wide on the pristine grass. A backdrop of tall redwoods surrounded the entire campus, giving the impression that the car was entering a secret emerald-green forest retreat, with the trees' canopy forming a secure border perfectly outlined against a vivid blue sky.

Joy tried to take in the scenery, but she was still worried about the console. If they were careful, everything would be fine, she told herself. Plus being around Grace and Bree always gave Riley a mood boost.

"You guys, I'm *so* psyched!" Grace exclaimed.

"Me too!" Bree replied.

Riley beamed. "How great is next year gonna be? Coach Roberts's team has been state champs, like, every year!" She scrolled through her phone for a moment and then showed Bree and Grace a picture of a tall, confident girl with wavy hair that had a streak of iconic Fire Hawk red running through it. "And Val Ortiz is the captain now!"

"This Valentina Ortiz obsession is out of control," Anger said, rolling his eyes.

But regardless of Anger's opinion, Valentina Ortiz (Val for short) was Riley's hero. Riley didn't know Val. But Val's hockey prowess was the stuff of legend at Bridgeview Middle School. Valentina Ortiz had made the varsity team as a freshman. Her moves on the ice were unparalleled, and her slap shots were rumored to go one hundred miles per hour. But above all that, Val exuded *cool.* Real Fire Hawks material.

"All we have to do is be super awesome at camp,"

Riley said. "Coach will put us on the team, and we'll all be Fire Hawks!"

At that, Bree and Grace shared a look.

Disgust's eyes narrowed. "Wait. What was that?"

"What was what?" asked Joy.

"We got a look," said Disgust. "I don't like this."

"What? You're paranoid," Joy said dismissively.

"I never miss a look," Disgust asserted.

She hit a button, prompting a miniature workstation to rise from the floor. She recalled the memory and paused on Bree's face. "Enhance fifteen to thirty-three," she commanded. "Track forty-five right. Zoom in." The computer zoomed in on Bree's eyebrow.

"See? Right there!" Disgust exclaimed, pointing at the image. Bree's eyebrow had raised a tenth of an inch.

"So?" Anger asked, confused.

Disgust didn't take her eyes off the screen. "She's hiding something! But what?" After a moment, she nodded. "Only one way to find out."

Disgust tapped a button, causing Riley to make the tiniest expression change.

Bree stared at Riley, the two in a silent standoff. Grace's eyes darted back and forth between her two friends. Finally, she couldn't take it anymore.

"Coach Roberts isn't going to be our coach next year!" Grace blurted out.

Bree smacked Grace on the shoulder and gave her an admonishing look.

"We . . . got assigned to a different high school," Bree finally admitted.

"Aha!" Disgust exclaimed. Then it sunk in. "Oh. Oh, no . . ."

"This is a *huge* deal!" Fear exclaimed.

"We can't go to high school without Bree and Grace!" said Anger.

"We won't know anybody," Sadness whimpered.

"Oh, okay," Riley began, trying to hide the chaos of her Emotions. "No big deal."

"We'll still get to hang out," Bree said.

"And we'll have this weekend?" Grace's voice was more questioning than reassuring. "Which means we'll get one last time playing on the same team?"

"Friends are forever, right?" Bree held out her hand to fist-bump Riley.

Not knowing how else to respond, Riley fist-bumped Bree and Grace, like she always did. "Yeah, of course."

"Oh, this is *so sad*!" Sadness lunged for the console.

"Wait, Sadness!" All the Emotions rushed to block her.

"Touchy console!"

"Don't do it!"

"You can't!"

"Just hold on until they're out of the car!" Disgust pleaded. They couldn't let Bree and Grace see Riley turn into a blubbering pile of tears. Then they really *wouldn't* want to be best friends anymore.

The Emotions watched, with Sadness still straining and sobbing, as the family car pulled up to the drop-off area.

"Here we are!" Dad said. "Wow, it looks pretty cool. You sure you don't need an assistant coach? I'm available."

Disgust rolled her eyes.

"Bill," Riley's mom chided him.

"Okay, okay. We'll see you in a few days," Riley's dad said.

"Thanks for the ride!" Bree and Grace hopped out of the car.

Sadness welled up with a fresh wave of anguish. It took everything the Emotions had to restrain her.

Riley hesitated for a moment but then started to follow her friends.

"Honey, hold on," Riley's mom said. "Are you sure you have everything? Stick?"

"Yes," Riley replied.

"Gloves?"

"Yes," Riley repeated, more annoyed now.

"What's with the interrogation?" Anger complained.

"They're worried," Sadness said, still trying to push her way to the console. "We can cry in front of them."

"No! Then they may not let Riley stay at camp," said Joy. "Just give it a few more seconds, until Riley is alone."

"You have your phone?" Riley's dad asked.

"Yes, of course," Riley replied.

"Okay, call us if you need us," Riley's dad said. "I love you. Go get 'em."

"Okay, love you guys," Riley said as she hopped out of the car.

"Don't forget your deodorant!" her mom called.

"Mom!" Riley exclaimed. She looked around to make sure no one had heard.

"Bye, monkey!" her dad added.

Riley closed the door and watched as they drove away.

Finally, the Emotions released their grip on Sadness, and she collapsed against the console, turning it a rippling blue. Riley burst into tears.

Joy put a hand on Sadness's shoulder. "It's okay. We need this."

Still crying, Riley turned around only to realize that some girls were standing right in front of her.

Sadness gasped and stepped away from the console.

"We can't cry in front of our peers!" Disgust exclaimed in horror.

Fear trembled. "There are so many people to make a bad first impression on!"

Joy couldn't let their negativity continue. "It's okay. We'll have plenty of time to think about this after camp. We just need to find Bree and Grace."

She turned to the console.

"We get one last hurrah with our besties," Joy said, more to herself than the others. "And we're going to make the most of it."

EMBARRASSMENT • ENNUI • ENVY • FEAR • JOY • SADNESS • ANGER • ANXIETY • DISGUST

Chapter 9

Riley quickly wiped away her tears as she scanned the group of teenagers filtering into the camp. She didn't recognize anyone; all these girls were high schoolers. The way they chatted and strode into the camp like they knew exactly where to go made Riley feel small and alone. Had Bree and Grace gone inside already?

I guess they have each other, she thought bitterly. *Why would they need me?* Riley knew she was being harsh. Part of her understood it wasn't Bree and Grace's fault they got assigned to a different high school. But they could have at least given her a heads-up. Now here she was standing in a crowd of strangers and wondering what she was going to do as a high school freshman with no friends. Meanwhile, Bree and Grace were wherever they were—*not* worrying about that.

Finally, she spotted them in the distance. She began to rush over when . . .

BAM!

She collided with another person and fell on her butt.

"Gah!" Riley exclaimed, rubbing her tailbone.

"Whoa—are you okay?"

Riley looked up at the person she'd whacked into—and she gasped.

She couldn't believe it.

It was Valentina Ortiz.

She had smacked into Valentina Ortiz—and landed on her butt. Riley stared agape, with no words coming out.

Valentina took Riley's hand to help her up. "Hey, hi. My name's Valentina."

"I know!" Riley's voice squeaked with a higher pitch than usual. "You're the varsity captain. You set the all-time goal record as a junior. Your favorite color is red, and your skate size is nine and a half—just like me!"

O.M.G. *What* was she saying?

Luckily, Val didn't seem weirded out. Instead, she smiled. "Oh! You're the one Coach told us about. Riley from Michigan, right?"

Riley could barely keep her thoughts straight.

This was Valentina Ortiz—*the* Valentina Ortiz. Talking to her! And Val had *heard* of her! Sure, Val had gotten the state wrong, but Riley wasn't sure she was supposed to correct her. What if she embarrassed Val? Or sounded like a know-it-all? No, no, no—she couldn't do that.

"Yeah," Riley said, laughing nervously. "That's me. Riley from good old Michigan."

"What are we saying?" Disgust smacked her head, still gagging from Riley's stalker-level list of random Valentina Ortiz facts.

"We are so uncool," Sadness said, shaking her head.

"Why are we still holding her hand?" Fear flailed in a panic.

"And why didn't Riley tell her the truth?" Joy's brow furrowed. "We're not from Michigan."

Suddenly, the console glowed bright orange.

"Orange?" Joy asked. "Who made the console orange?"

She looked at the others one by one. They all shook their heads.

"Do I look orange?" Anger asked, irked.

"I didn't touch it!" Fear insisted.

"Orange is *not* my color," Disgust said.

"Not me," Sadness added.

"But then, who . . ." Joy turned to look back at the console—and came face to face with a bizarre-looking creature she had never seen before.

"Hello, everybody!" the creature exclaimed.

"Ahhhh!" the Emotions all screamed at once. Fear, Sadness, Disgust, and Anger ran and hid behind Joy.

The orange creature scooted closer, with a bounce in her step so peppy she was borderline vibrating. She was short and wiry, with bugged-out eyes and a shock of hair that stuck straight up atop her head. She tugged nervously at the striped turtleneck rolled beneath her wide chin and mouth.

"Oh my gosh, I am just such a *huge* fan of yours! And now here I am meeting you face to face! Okay, how can I help?" she said.

"Uhhh . . ." Joy and the others were very, *very* unsettled. What was going on? Since when were there visitors to HQ? Mind Workers came and went occasionally. But this was no Mind Worker.

"I can take notes," the newcomer said as she whipped out a pen and pad from her deep-pocketed brown pants.

"Get coffee? Manage your calendar? Walk your dog? Carry your things? Watch you sleep?"

"Wow!" Joy said uncertainly. "You . . . have a lot of energy. Maybe you could just stay where I can see you."

"Anything!" the creature exclaimed. "Just call my name, and I am here for you."

"And . . . what was your name again?" Joy asked.

"Oh! I'm sorry. I can get ahead of myself. I'm Anxiety. I'm one of Riley's new Emotions!" She puffed out her chest proudly, though she was still vibrating a little. Joy could tell because her stringy stalk of hair was quavering. "And we are just super jazzed to be here."

"Wait, what do you mean 'we'?" Disgust asked.

Suddenly, a tiny blue-green hand crept up, trying to reach the buttons on the console. "I wish I was as tall as all of you," the owner of the hand whined.

"Ahh!" Joy and the others jumped back. There were more weird Emotions invading HQ!

This one was pint-sized, with big puppy dog eyes and a head too large for her body. Her wavy teal hair stuck out in messy poofs like a preschooler's.

"Who the heck are *you?*" Anger asked.

"I'm Envy," the new Emotion said. She gave each of

them an unsettlingly sweet grin before spotting Disgust's sleek green hair. "Oooh." She reached out to touch it. "Look at your hair . . ."

Disgust whacked her little hand away. "Not happening."

Envy turned her attention to the screen, where Val was still talking with Riley. Envy's wide eyes grew even wider. "Oooh—look at *her* hair." She admired Val's wavy brown locks with a streak of red running through them. "We need hair like that!"

Before anyone could stop her, Envy pressed a button on the console. On-screen, Riley reached out toward Val's hair. "Oh my gosh, I love the red in your hair!"

"Oh, I—" Val pulled back awkwardly from Riley's attempt to touch her hair.

"What are you doing?" Disgust cried, horrified. She snatched Envy away from the console. "We don't just *touch* people!"

Riley shuffled, realizing she'd messed up. "Hey, maybe when I make the team, I can join Team Red Head, too! Yeah, yeah!" She gave a weak fist pump.

Joy and the other core Emotions cringed. This wasn't like their girl at all!

Suddenly, the console lit up with a pink glow.

"Now what?" Anger fumed, turning to see yet another

new Emotion standing in HQ. Unlike Envy, this one was massive. He had a squishy pink body stuffed into a mauve fleece hoodie. His nose was so big and round it looked like a marshmallow stuck to his face. And his oversized sweaty palms were all over the console, turning it pink.

Riley's cheeks flushed as she fumbled for words. "Sorry, that was a totally dorky thing to say."

"Okay, who's this guy?" Anger demanded.

The looming pink Emotion pulled the drawstrings of his hoodie tighter, closing the hood around his face so that only his eyes peeked out.

"What's your name, big fella?" Sadness asked.

"That's Embarrassment!" Anxiety popped up out of nowhere—again. "He's not big on eye contact or, uh, like, talking. But he's a really sweet guy."

"Well, welcome to Headquarters, Embarrassment!" Joy tried to shake hands with him, but Embarrassment went for a fist bump instead. He blushed a deeper pink.

Meanwhile, Val was offering to show Riley the way into camp. "Hey, do you want to come with me, actually?" she said. "You can meet some of the other Fire Hawks."

Anxiety started vibrating with eager energy. "Oooh! This is exciting! But we can't let her know we're excited."

The console suddenly glowed deep purple, and Riley

pretended to be nonchalant about Val's offer. "Yeah, sounds good."

"What Emotion was that?" Anger asked, more confused than ever.

"That's Ennui," Anxiety said.

"Enn-what?" Joy raised an eyebrow.

The Emotions all turned to where a long droopy purple Emotion was lying on the couch, scrolling on her phone. She gave a deeply annoyed sigh.

"It's pronounced *ON-WEE*," Ennui corrected Joy in her French accent. "It's what you would call the 'boredom.'"

Joy looked at the others and shrugged. This Emotion had a chip on her shoulder.

"Well, come on up here, Ennn-wuuur? Am I saying it right? En-waa. No," Joy said.

Ennui did not respond.

"Oh, nicknames!" Joy tried to salvage the situation. "I'm going to call you Wee-wee!"

Ennui didn't look up from her phone. *"Non."*

The console glowed purple once more even though Ennui wasn't touching it.

"How are you driving?" Fear asked.

Ennui held up her phone, displaying a picture of the console. "Console app."

Anger couldn't hold back any longer. "Hey! Stop it! That's enough!"

"Now, now," said Joy, "I know new Emotions can sometimes feel unhelpful at first, and you just wanna say to them, 'Why are you so annoying?' " She put her arm around Sadness a little too tightly. "But I've learned that every Emotion is good for Riley. Even this turkey." She squeezed Sadness again.

Joy didn't fully trust these new Emotions, but she didn't want to repeat the mistakes she had made with Sadness.

Anger shrugged. "Okay, fine."

With Ennui driving the console once more, Riley picked up her bag and tossed it over her shoulder. "Lead the way," she told Val.

"Oh, but what about our friends?" Sadness said.

The Emotions could see Bree and Grace nearby on-screen. Bree and Grace didn't see Riley, though. Riley paused as she decided what to do.

"Val is our future," Envy said simply.

Anxiety nodded vigorously. "Yes, I agree completely. We need new friends, or we'll be totally alone in high school! Right, Joy?"

"Well, um, actually . . ." Joy started.

"Great!" Anxiety exclaimed. She began driving.

Riley hurried after Val. "Wait up! Thanks for showing me around!"

Joy gasped. "Why did you do that?"

"Oh, no, sorry!" Anxiety whipped her hands away from the buttons like a kid who had been caught doing something naughty. "What did I do?"

Joy gave her a perturbed look. What did she mean? She knew exactly what she'd done. "We just left our best friends behind."

"But what about the new ones that we're about to meet?" Anxiety asked, confused.

Behind her, Envy, Embarrassment, and Ennui nodded.

Joy stared at them. Bree and Grace were Riley's best friends for life. They brought out the best in Riley. Anxiety couldn't toss that all away for people they barely knew.

"What? No!" Joy said incredulously. "These next three days need to be about Bree and Grace."

Anxiety's expression changed. "Joy," she said in a serious tone, "the next three days could determine the next *four years* of our lives."

"I think that's overstating things a bit," Joy said.

To Joy's surprise, the new Emotions snickered.

"Ooh la la. Joy is so old-school," Ennui said mockingly.

"What?" Joy said, rather offended, though she wasn't sure what Ennui even meant.

"Look, Joy," Anxiety said, "we all have a job to do. You make Riley happy. Sadness makes her sad. Fear protects her from the scary stuff she can see. And *my* job is to protect her from the scary stuff she *can't* see. I plan for the future. Here, let me show you."

Anxiety touched an indentation in the console, causing a screen to pop up through it.

"Oh, that's what that does," Sadness said, surprised.

"I was using that as a cup holder," Joy added under her breath.

"Okay, so my team has run all the data, and we're looking at the following likely scenarios." Anxiety began tapping the screen, showing projections of things that could happen to Riley in the future. "First, we don't take this camp seriously and we goof off with Bree and Grace." An image of Riley, Grace, and Bree acting silly appeared. "Riley looks really uncool in front of Val. She fails to impress Coach." The image switched to Coach kicking Riley out of camp while all the older girls laughed at her. "She does *not* become a Fire Hawk and finally arrives at high school with no one. She eats alone, and only the teachers know her name." A final image popped up of Riley, sad and alone, sitting at a high school cafeteria table.

"Ew." Disgust recoiled.

"Okay, you and I are going to be friends," Fear said, impressed.

"Oh, this is a sad story," Sadness said, getting teary-eyed.

"It's a *ridiculous* story," Joy said. Who did this newbie think she was, projecting all these horrible thoughts into Riley's head? It was time to get things back under control.

"Again, I love the energy," Joy said authoritatively, pulling rank, "but you're being silly. *None* of this will actually happen."

Joy's tone must have worked, because Anxiety began fidgeting like a student who had been told they were out of line. "Right, right." She switched off the projection screen. "Whatever you say. You're the boss."

Chapter 10

Riley followed Val closely down the winding halls and into the locker room of the ice rink. She tried to take some deep, calming breaths, but she couldn't stop shaking. Why was she so nervous?

It's just hockey practice like normal, Riley thought, trying to convince herself.

But obviously it wasn't. This was Coach Roberts's varsity skills camp. And though the locker room was pungent with the familiar musty smell of skates, sweat, and bleach, as soon as Riley stepped through the red double doors and saw all the self-assured high school students unpacking their gear, talking and laughing like they'd been there their whole lives, she felt a pang of longing for *her* familiar locker room and *her* familiar faces at the Foghorns' training sessions. Maybe she should have waited for Bree and Grace after all. Things didn't feel the same without them.

Luckily, Val didn't seem to notice how nervous Riley was. "Come on!" Val said cheerfully. "I want you to meet the other Fire Hawks."

She led Riley to a group of girls lacing up their skates. Each had a streak of red in her hair, like Val.

"Hey, what's up?" the girls said, nodding in Riley's direction.

"Hey." Riley waved meekly. These girls were *so* cool. She tried to picture herself sitting there by that time next year, lacing up her skates and confidently shooting passing teammates a "what's up?" nod, with a streak of red running through her own sandy-blond hair.

"Riley is from Michigan," Val told the other girls.

Gah! Riley *really* couldn't correct Val now—not in front of the other Fire Hawks. She guessed Michigan was her new, unofficial home state.

"Oh, cool." A Fire Hawk with cropped brown hair and an eyebrow piercing snapped her gum. "Where in Michigan are you from?"

"Uh . . ." Riley gulped. *Think fast—think fast!* "I'm from . . . all over."

"Nice," the girl said. "I've got a cousin in Minneapolis."

"Cool." Riley nodded, knowing full well that Minneapolis was in Minnesota, not Michigan—because *she* was from Minnesota, not Michigan.

"Dani, that's *Minnesota*," another Fire Hawk said, correcting her. "Two completely different states."

Riley felt sweat pooling under her arms.

"Hey, you want to sit with us?" Val motioned to an empty space on the bench.

"She wants to sit with us! Everything is beautiful!" Anxiety cheered. She pushed Joy toward the console.

Joy shot her a look. "There's not enough room for Bree and Grace." She saw an empty bench nearby. "Oh! We should go sit over there."

"Oh, sorry . . ." Riley said to Val. "I was going to go save seats for my friends."

Val shrugged. "Oh, okay. It's cool."

Riley headed to the empty bench and put her bag down.

"See? Was that so hard?" Joy said.

Beside her, the little orange Emotion vibrated vigorously, and Anxiety's left eye twitched. "No, that was super great."

Riley saw Bree and Grace hurrying into the locker room. "Bree! Grace!" She waved, motioning them to the bench.

"There you are!" Grace said. "We lost sight of you!"

Riley hugged her friends, and the three of them laughed happily.

"Time to celebrate!" Joy exclaimed, hitting a button on the console.

"Say *'ahhh-woooga'*!" Riley exclaimed, doing the Celly Dance with her friends.

"AHHH-WOOOGA!" the three girls cheered, snapping silly selfies with their phones.

There was a murmur in the locker room as a heavy door closed somewhere.

"Okay, ladies, let's all settle in." Coach Roberts's voice came from off-screen. She didn't sound very celebratory.

"Uh . . . Joy?" Anxiety warned her.

But Joy was too busy driving the console and keeping the party going to notice. "Aw, yeah!" she said, laughing.

"Skills camp selfies!" Riley made a peace sign with her fingers, snapping another photo of her, Bree, and Grace.

"Ladies, 'settle in' means settle down." Coach's voice

was sterner. "I need your focus." She came into view on the screen in front of Riley and looked with distaste at her phone, the source of the distraction. "Which means now I'm going to need your cell phones. All of them."

The players groaned.

"What?"

"Thanks, new girl."

"Are you serious?"

They shut their mouths when Coach Roberts glanced their way.

"You're here to work. Not to goof around." Coach Roberts turned to Riley. "Got that, Andersen?"

Inside HQ, Embarrassment lumbered forward and leaned heavily on the console.

"Yes, Coach." Riley turned beet red.

Coach Roberts collected everyone's phones in a basket while several players continued muttering under their breath.

Next to Riley, Grace whispered, "Wow. Coach is so serious."

"Aw, see?" Joy smiled. "Grace gets us. Besties always understand."

Joy nudged Embarrassment's squishy arm over a bit, mingling a hint of yellow with the pink on the console.

"Uh, Joy, maybe I could help a little . . ." Anxiety tugged at her turtleneck.

"Thank you, not now," Joy replied.

The gold spread, and they heard Riley whisper to Grace, "I know, right?"

The two of them giggled, catching Coach's attention again.

"Oh, you think this is funny?" Coach shot them a withering look. "Well, you know what else is funny? Skating lines. Now hit the ice, ladies!"

Once again, everyone in the locker room groaned.

"Ugh!"

"Come on!"

"Thanks a lot, Michigan!"

Dani, the Fire Hawk with the eyebrow piercing, bumped into Riley on her way to the ice. "Nice, Andersen," she said, her tone now much less civil.

Ennui walked up beside Joy, who had finally removed her hands from the console, her expression stricken.

"Bravo, Joy," Ennui said. "Riley's *totally* fitting in now."

"Oh, thanks so much, Wee-wee," Joy snapped sarcastically.

Chapter 11

Riley had never skated so hard in her life. She was no stranger to skating lines. But seeing as she was the one who had gotten the whole team into trouble, she figured it was up to her to show Coach that she *was* taking camp seriously. No more messing around for Riley Andersen. Somehow she had to turn this around.

The whole time, she heard the other high school players grumbling, "This is the worst," and "What a way to start camp." Riley began to wonder if she had already completely messed up camp—perhaps even her entire high school existence. But she pushed the thought away and instead skated harder.

At least Bree and Grace didn't hate her for making them skate lines. *They* knew it wasn't Riley's fault.

But then again, Bree and Grace wouldn't be there to back her up in high school the next year, would they?

Coach Roberts finally blew her whistle. "All right, ladies. Take a breather! Then we'll divide into teams."

Exhausted, Riley exited the rink, then caught her breath beside the stadium seats.

That was when she heard it: "Oof. That Michigan girl is off to a rough start."

Riley gasped. She peeked through the stair railing, careful to stay out of sight. Some of the Fire Hawks were sitting together, drinking from water bottles.

"I'd heard good things about her. But now I don't know what to think."

The girls shrugged, and Riley, flushing crimson, felt heat in her cheeks.

Were they talking about *her*?

"Oh, no . . ." Anxiety looked like she was about to throw up. "Are they talking about *us*?"

The Emotions watched, stunned, from Riley's vantage point behind the railing.

"Coach isn't going to put her on the team if she can't get it together," Dani said, chuckling, and popped a fresh piece of gum in her mouth.

"What's that hotshot think is so funny?" Anger fumed.

"Oh, right, Dani." Val rolled her eyes. "Like you had it all together when you were a freshman?"

"Come on," Dani protested. "I wasn't *that* immature."

Inside HQ, Embarrassment let out a strangled gasp. He collapsed spectacularly across the console, practically melting into the board and hitting with his massive marshmallow body every button possible—except one.

"Oh, I got you, big guy," Sadness offered. She pressed the last button.

Hot tears of humiliation burned Riley's eyes. Her chest heaved.

"I always wanted people to talk about us, but not like this!" Envy whined.

"Oh, Joy, what do we do now?" Sadness asked.

Everyone turned to Joy, who could feel the heat of uncertainty creeping up inside her as well.

"Um . . . we can just—We're fine . . ."

"Fine?" Ennui huffed. "This is a disaster."

"I have an idea!" Anxiety popped up beside Joy, startling her for what seemed like the umpteenth time. "If we can get Val on our side, everything will be okay!"

Out of nowhere, Anxiety held up an idea light bulb and slotted it into the console. Instantly, it lit up.

Wiping her eyes, Riley took a deep breath. All the Fire Hawks had headed to the locker room except for Val, who sat on the bleachers, adjusting her skates.

"Uh, Val . . ." Riley started nervously.

Val looked up. "Oh, hey, Riley." She sounded awkward.

"I'm just—" Riley was so embarrassed and miserable she felt like she was falling apart. She just wanted Val to like her again. "I'm so sorry. I didn't mean to get the whole team skating lines. I feel terrible. I respect you so much. And I would never do anything to mess it up. You're a great hockey player, and you lead the team so amazingly, and I really look up to you and—"

"Okay, okay." Val let out a small laugh and held up her hand to stop Riley's effusive praise. "Thanks. Listen, Coach was hard on you today. But that's not a bad thing. It means you're on her radar."

A glimmer of hope rose in Riley.

"Really?" she asked.

Val stood. "Hey, I'm glad you came to talk with me. Let's try to be on the same team later, okay?"

Riley nodded, feeling a tiny bit better. "Oh, yeah! Cool."

She took a shaky breath. Maybe she could turn things around after all.

CHAPTER 11

Inside HQ, the new Emotions clapped.

"Good job. Wow." Ennui looked pleased despite herself.

"Now that was . . . yes, wow," Fear agreed. "How did you do that?"

Envy reached up to touch the edge of Anxiety's sweater. "I wish I could do that!"

"Aw, you guys," Anxiety said sheepishly. "I mean, it really wasn't anything. I'm just trying to help."

Joy watched as the new Emotions nodded in agreement and even the core Emotions seemed to be considering Anxiety's strategy. She didn't like this. It didn't feel right. It didn't feel like it was best for Riley.

"I agree. Great job, Anxiety," Joy said, ushering the vibrating orange Emotion away from the console. "I stepped back, you stepped in, you got Riley back on track, now I'm ready to step back in—"

"Oh, uh, but that was just part one of my plan," Anxiety said, interrupting her.

"There's a part two?" Joy asked. She was getting a bad feeling about this.

"A good plan has many parts, Joy," Anxiety said.

Chapter 12

"Okay, ladies!" Coach Roberts blew her whistle as everyone filtered back onto the ice. "We're going to form your teams for the rest of camp. Split yourselves down the middle—Team One on the right, Team Two on the left."

Riley stood off to the side, cold sweat making her uniform damp and uncomfortably sticky under her protective padding. *Everything will be okay,* she kept telling herself. *Val wants me on her team. So that's a win. I'll be with the Fire Hawks and show them that I'm serious, and then they'll know I'm cool and not a loser—*

"Hey, Riley!" Bree and Grace skated up behind her.

Gah! Riley mentally smacked herself. She'd been so focused on Val she'd completely forgotten she had promised to be on the same team as Bree and Grace.

"Oh, hey . . ." she started.

"Let's do this!" Bree energetically held out her knuckles for a fist bump.

"One more time on the same team, right?" Grace grinned.

"Right . . ." Riley said hesitantly. She turned to look at Val, who was lining up with the other Fire Hawks. "Hey, let's join Team One," she said hopefully.

"Nah, they're full." Grace nodded to the other group of girls, gathering on the left. "Let's go over on this side."

Riley's heart started to beat faster as she did a quick mental count of Team One. *Ugh, hockey sticks!* Grace was right. They had room for only one more player if the teams were going to be even.

"Come on!" Bree said, leading the way toward Team Two.

Riley looked longingly at Team One. Val was motioning for her to join them.

Riley stood, paralyzed, in the center of the ice.

She had to choose.

What was she going to do?

"Val wants us!" Envy whined, jumping up and down beside the console like a toddler who couldn't reach the countertop.

"But we promised Bree and Grace!" Joy insisted.

Anxiety's left eye twitched. "Joy, we have to let go of the past." Before Joy could stop her, Anxiety quickly tapped on the console. But something strange happened: the console didn't respond.

"Come on, Riley. Move!" Anxiety's voice shook. "Move those feet! Val's on Team One. You want to be on Team One. Let's go!"

When the console still didn't respond, Anxiety changed tactics and tapped the projection screen, bringing up an image of Riley playing with the Fire Hawks. A streak of red ran through her perfectly pulled-back hair. "Look! If we can use this camp to befriend the Fire Hawks, high school will be amazing!"

Still, Riley didn't move. She remained frozen in the center of the ice. The teams were fully formed except for an open spot remaining on Team One. Bree and Grace were waving for Riley to join them. Another player on Team Two noticed and began to shift toward Team One, making space for Riley so the teams would be even.

Val gave Riley a confused look, one that said, *Are you coming or not?* It was now or never.

"She made a promise to her friends," Joy said confidently. This newbie might know a few nifty tricks, but she clearly didn't know their girl the way Joy did. "She's not going to break it."

Anxiety's hands stopped tapping the console. She stood very still.

"You're so right, Joy," she said.

Without another word, Anxiety walked over to the Sense of Self, grasped it, and yanked it off the base.

Everyone gasped as the light emanating from Headquarters dimmed and receded.

"What are you doing?" Joy cried, beside herself.

Riley, now with a blank and indifferent expression, turned to skate toward Val.

Joy sprinted at Anxiety and grabbed the Sense of Self. "No! You can't have that! Put that back!"

The two Emotions struggled over the Sense of Self until Joy pried it out of Anxiety's hands and placed it back on the pedestal. "*This* is Riley."

Riley's expression changed to concern as she turned to skate toward Bree and Grace instead.

Joy sighed in relief. Their girl was back.

"No, Joy!" Anxiety exclaimed. "I don't mean to overstep, but it has to be done."

Before Joy could stop her, Anxiety zipped past and pulled the Sense of Self off the pedestal again. She lowered the Back of the Mind tube and loaded the Sense of Self inside.

"Stop!" Joy shouted, desperately scrambling to reach her. "No! Don't!"

But it was too late. Anxiety pulled back the plunger and launched Riley's Sense of Self into the farthest reaches of her mind.

Joy sank to her knees. Sadness, Anger, Disgust, and Fear were too shocked and horrified to know what to say or do.

"No . . ." Joy whimpered.

Anxiety turned back to the console. "I know change is scary, but—but watch!"

Riley finally skated to Team One and stood in their ranks.

"Riley?" Bree and Grace, clearly hurt, stared at her.

"Teams all formed?" Coach Roberts called. "All right, let's get going."

Val smiled and put an arm around Riley's shoulders in a genuinely kind way, almost like she was taking her under her wing. "Welcome to our team, Michigan."

"That is *not* Riley!" Joy shouted, practically shaking with rage. For once she understood how Anger felt all the time.

"I know! It's a better Riley!" Anxiety's tone was elated, like she had just figured out the solution to all their problems. "We build her a new Sense of Self. A brand-new her!"

"A Riley who won't be alone next year!" Envy added. She scurried to the elevator platform and pressed the buttons to call the Belief System elevator to HQ. The double doors slid open.

Meanwhile, Anxiety walked over to the wall where fresh memory spheres were rolling in. She selected an orange one and replayed the memory of Val telling Riley she should join her team. She moved toward the elevator with the memory sphere in her hands.

"Whoa, whoa, whoa," Joy said. "Put that back! You can't go down there with that!"

She and the other core Emotions blocked Anxiety's path to the elevator.

"Over my dead flaming body!" Anger added for good measure.

Anxiety studied each of them. Her expression had gone strangely grim.

"I am truly sorry," she said at last. "I was so looking forward to working with you guys." She nodded to Embarrassment, and the hulking pink Emotion walked over and scooped up Joy and her friends in one fell swoop.

"Hey!" Joy struggled against Embarrassment's squishy yet strong arms. "What do you think you're doing?"

"Riley's life is more complex now," Anxiety continued matter-of-factly. "It requires more sophisticated Emotions than all of you. You just aren't what she needs anymore, Joy."

Joy felt as though she'd been hit in the stomach.

"How dare you, madam!" Fear exclaimed, sounding angrier than he had, well, ever.

"You can't just bottle us up!" Joy countered.

At that, Anxiety smiled. "Oh! That's a great idea!"

Anxiety called the Mind Police, and minutes later, several officers brought in a gigantic glass jar. Joy's stomach plummeted with a sickening feeling. Anxiety was going to bottle them up—literally.

"Wait!" Joy exclaimed, distraught. "No! You can't do this!"

"Where did those guys come from?" Anger fumed.

"Where did they even *find* that?" Disgust asked.

But Anxiety offered no explanations. She simply motioned for Embarrassment to do her bidding. The lumbering Emotion tossed Joy and her friends inside the jar, closed the lid, and poked a few air holes in the top. The Mind cops pushed the jar to the construction lift outside the windows of HQ.

"It's not forever," said Anxiety. "It's just until Riley makes varsity or until she turns eighteen. Or—or maybe forever. I don't know! We'll see!"

"She's all set," one of the cops said into a walkie-talkie. "Lower her down."

On command, the construction lift began lowering the jar to the ground.

The Emotions shouted in protest.

"Stop!"

"Let us out!"

"We don't belong here!"

"You can't do this, Anxiety!"

But within moments, they were gone.

Envy, Embarrassment, and Ennui looked at each other nervously. HQ suddenly seemed large and empty with just the four new Emotions left.

"Let Operation: New Riley begin," Anxiety announced.

She cradled the orange memory sphere. "Don't worry, Riley," she said reassuringly, watching the memory with Val replaying over and over. "You're in good hands." She stepped toward the elevator.

Ding!

The elevator doors whooshed open. The four new Emotions pushed and jostled their way out of the tight space into the cavernous Belief System.

"Okay, next time we take two trips," Ennui said, stretching and massaging her long arms.

Embarrassment stared in awe at the expanse of beautiful belief strings and memories. He plucked one of the strings.

I'm kind.

Embarrassment smiled. He was certain that was one of his favorite beliefs.

Envy wanted to know more about Anxiety's plan. "How do we build a new Riley if it took the other Emotions thirteen years to build the old one?"

"Well, the good news is we're not starting from scratch," Anxiety said, gesturing to the existing belief strings.

She didn't want to change Riley completely. Many of these beliefs made Riley the special person she was. But to Anxiety, there was always room for improvement. "And the better news is that Joy taught us how to cheat the system."

She held the orange memory sphere and knelt next to the pool.

"One belief at a time," she murmured.

"I wanna plant one," Envy whined.

"Next time," Anxiety said, placing the memory into the water. An orange belief string sprouted from the memory sphere and attached to the larger system.

"By the time we're done with this place, you won't even recognize it," Anxiety said. She plucked the new belief.

If I'm a Fire Hawk, I won't be alone.

Orange light pulsed from the Belief System up to the base of Headquarters. The other belief strings flickered. Anxiety knew if they had enough beliefs, the orange light would eventually envelop all of Headquarters. It would then lead to a new Sense of Self and a new Riley, who would be prepared for high school.

Anxiety couldn't wait to get started.

Chapter 13

Every muscle in Riley's body ached. There were muscles she'd never known she had that ached, thanks to one of the hardest training sessions she had ever been through in her life. Her misguided giggle in the locker room was a distant memory after the intense drills Coach Roberts had put them through. There was no doubt skills camp meant business, and those high school girls were *tough*. Every single Fire Hawk seemed to know how to perform complex maneuvers like they'd been born with skates on their feet.

And yet . . . Riley had done okay, she thought. She'd run every single drill they had, and she'd even helped set up a goal for Dani once. It had been hard, but at least she hadn't caused the players to have to skate lines anymore. Coach Roberts had even nodded approvingly in her direction at one point. That had to count for something, right?

The locker room was mostly empty now, except for a few players from Team Two who were finishing packing up their stuff. Bree and Grace were nowhere in sight. Riley breathed a small sigh of relief. She felt terrible remembering the looks of disappointment on their faces when she'd chosen Val's team instead of theirs. They hadn't said a word to her for the rest of practice.

Riley slung her bag over her shoulder and pushed through the red double doors.

"Hey! Riley!"

Uh-oh. Grace was standing there, with her arms crossed over her chest. Bree was next to her. They both looked upset, and Riley was pretty sure they'd been talking about her.

"Oh, hey, guys," Riley said.

Grace frowned. "Why did you do that?"

"Hmmm. They do not sound *très* happy," Ennui commented as she collapsed onto the couch.

The Emotions had returned to Headquarters from their quick field trip to the Belief System just in time.

Anxiety took a deep breath. Bree's and Grace's looks of confusion, disappointment, and betrayal were hard to ignore. She didn't want to hurt them—really, she didn't. Was this too harsh? Would they hate Riley forever?

Envy scurried to the console with a little step stool she'd made out of construction debris and used it to hop up so she could see. "What should we do?"

Anxiety tapped on the projection screen, bringing up the image of Riley skating with the Fire Hawks in high school. A streak of red ran through her hair. She looked happy and proud. More importantly, she looked like she *belonged.*

The one and only *Valentina Ortiz* had invited them to be on her team. How were they supposed to say no to that? It wasn't like they would have anyone else looking out for them at their new high school. This was their only option.

"We stay focused. We have bigger and better plans now," Anxiety said.

"Oooh." Envy watched the projection hungrily. "I like that."

On-screen, Bree had her arms crossed. "We all agreed to play on the same team. We fist-bumped. You never go back on a fist bump."

"I know," Riley replied. "It's just . . . Val asked me to join her team—"

"'Val'?" Grace raised an eyebrow. "What, are you guys on a nickname basis now?"

"Yeah, kind of." Riley bristled. "She's actually really nice."

"But this was supposed to be our last chance to play together," Bree insisted.

"You really left us hanging there." Grace was clearly bitter.

"I just . . . I figured . . ." Riley was struggling to find the words.

Anxiety brought up the projection of Riley as a Fire Hawk once more, reminding Riley of their true goal.

"I just figured I should get some time in with the team I'll be playing with next year," Riley said finally.

"But, Riley, it's nearly impossible to get on varsity as a freshman," Bree said, her tone matter of fact.

Grace nodded. "I know you want to be a Fire Hawk. But let's be real. Valentina Ortiz is the exception, not the rule."

"Are they making fun of us?" Anxiety exclaimed.

"How can they call themselves our best friends if they don't even believe in us?"

"You think I can't?" Riley snapped.

Bree looked at Grace. "I think we wanted to all play together one last time."

"Let me handle this," Ennui said. Her fingers tapped away in a rapid-fire sequence on her phone.

"Whatever. I'm going to go get something to eat," Riley said. She started walking off toward the cafeteria, which was open late especially for the skills camp.

"Wait, Riley! Don't be like that. We'll come with you." Bree hurried to match Riley's pace, and Grace followed, though she shuffled her feet in doing so.

"Forget about the teams." Bree clearly wanted to smooth things over. "At least we're still here together, right?"

Riley looked straight ahead. "I guess."

"Hey, maybe there will be funnel cake in the cafeteria," said Bree. "Or blue slushy?" She nudged Grace. "You never know when Lizard Tongue will strike."

Riley recalled a memory from the Get Up and Glow concert, of Grace slurping up her slushy and sticking out her electric-blue tongue. For the past month, she'd burst into a fit of giggles every time she thought about it.

But right then, she couldn't even bring herself to smile.

Chapter 14

"Where are you putting us?" Fear wailed as two Mind cops pushed the glass jar containing all the core Emotions down a long darkened hallway. They passed door after door sealed with heavy metal padlocks, keeping whatever was inside from escaping.

"The same place we keep all of Riley's secrets," one of the cops said matter-of-factly. "The Vault."

"We're *not* secrets!" Fear protested.

"Oh, yeah, yeah, yeah. 'We're not secrets. You're making a big mistake,'" the other cop said, making air quotes with his fingers.

His partner chuckled. "Never heard that before."

They finally came to an open safe door deep within the Vault, and the Mind cops shoved the jar inside. They sealed the door shut with a resounding thunk.

And just like that, the Emotions were trapped in a

pitch-black room, locked away in the depths of Riley's mind with no escape.

"We are suppressed emotions!" Fear wailed, turning on his emergency flashlight.

All at once, the Emotions began to panic.

"Let us out right now!" Anger flared.

"We don't belong in a jar!" Disgust cried.

"Poor Riley!" Sadness wailed.

Joy, pushing aside the panic she, too, felt rising in her chest, motioned for everyone to calm down. "No, no, no! Riley's going to be fine! Totally fine!" *She has to be,* Joy thought desperately. *She has to be. She's our girl!*

"Hey there!" A singsongy voice echoed in the darkness. "Do you know what we call that? Denial! Can you say 'denial'?"

All the Emotions whipped around. Using his flashlight, Fear illuminated a bucktoothed purple cartoon dog wearing a ball cap and a fanny pack.

"Ahhhh!" the Emotions screamed.

"Hi, friends!" the cartoon dog said, giving them a big rainbow wave. "Welcome! It's so good to have you here with us today!"

"Wait . . ." Joy took a cautious step closer, squinting.

The dog looked familiar, like from a long-ago memory—one Riley hadn't recalled since she was in . . .

"It's Bloofy!" Joy realized with a laugh.

"From that preschool show Riley used to like?" Disgust asked.

Bloofy's bucktoothed grin grew wider. "That's *right*! And here's a little secret . . ." He leaned in closer to the jar. "Riley *still* likes the show."

The Emotions watched, dumbfounded, as Bloofy broke into a silly song and dance. *"Stomp like an elephant. Scurry like a mouse. Make your way down to Bloofy's house!"*

"Please kill me," Anger said.

"Bloofy!" Joy begged with renewed urgency. "We're in a real pickle! Could you help us get out of here?"

Bloofy turned to the blank safe wall and addressed it like it was an audience. "Uh-oh! We're going to need *your* help! Can *you* find a way out?"

"Who are you talking to?" Anger raised an eyebrow.

"My friends!" Bloofy gleefully gestured to the wall. He turned his attention back to his make-believe studio audience. "Do *you* see a key?" He paused for a long moment. "Hmm. I don't, either."

"Okay. We're doomed," said Fear.

Someone else spoke through the darkness. "Indeed. Welcome to your eternal fate."

Fear turned the flashlight onto a towering man with flowing dark magenta hair and piercing green eyes. He wore a warrior's tunic and gleaming shoulder armor, like an anime hero.

Disgust gasped. "Lance Slashblade?"

"But he's a video game character," Sadness pointed out. "Why is he here?"

Lance Slashblade wielded his massive hero's sword and struck a pose. His long hair billowed out behind him though there was no wind.

"Yeah, I always thought Riley had a secret crush on him," Disgust explained.

Joy shook her head. "I never saw the appeal."

Lance Slashblade clenched an anguished fist against his chest. "I long to be a hero," he proclaimed, his voice filled with unfathomable angst. "But darkness haunts my past."

"Oh, I get it." Anger nodded appreciatively.

"I'm in a hundred percent," Fear agreed.

"I just want to brush his hair," Disgust said with a sigh.

Without warning, a third voice emanated from

somewhere within the safe. But this was no ordinary voice. Instead of words, it rumbled a deep, unsettling growl.

"Uh . . ." Fear quavered. "Who's that?"

"Oh!" Bloofy did a happy little tap dance. "That's Riley's Deep Dark Secret."

The outline of an enormous hooded creature with glowing eyes appeared behind Lance Slashblade.

Fear whimpered. "What—what is the secret?"

Lance Slashblade shook his head. "You don't want to know."

"Riley's secrets!" Joy suddenly announced, trying to take back control. "A rogue Emotion has taken over Headquarters. Now, if you could just open the jar—"

Bloofy cut her off with a wag of his finger. "Hey, kids! Let's learn some Latin! Do you know 'quid pro quo'?" He chuckled. "We get you out of that jar. Then *you* get *us* out of this safe!"

"No, Bloofy." Lance Slashblade's voice held the weight of a thousand sorrows. "Their destiny is not ours to change. We were all banished here—deemed unfit. Worthless."

"Don't you dare say that!" Disgust pressed her hands against the glass jar and gazed at him. "You do not deserve to be thrown away!"

"Uh, one second, Lance," Joy said, pulling Disgust aside. "Don't you remember his power move?" she whispered.

"Well, yeah," Disgust admitted, recalling that Lance Slashblade's special video game move was rolling along the ground like a little balled-up hedgehog. Whenever Riley had used it, she had lost. "But it's not his fault!" Disgust insisted. "The Curse of the Wretched Roll was placed on him because the High Spirits were jealous that the underworld princess had entrusted the Immortal Slashblade to him!"

Disgust wheeled back to Lance Slashblade with her hands against her heart. "You listen to me, Lance Slashblade! No one is totally worthless!"

"But I am a warrior cursed with a feeble attack." Lance buried his perfectly angular face in his hands. His hair billowed out again in a nonexistent breeze.

"Then you must make your curse your gift!" Disgust implored him.

Lance looked up at her. Their eyes connected. A renewed determination lit his expression. He sheathed his sword and took an attack stance. "Shield yourselves, my friends. For I . . . shall set you all *free*!" he declared.

Everyone watched with bated breath as the legendary

hero dropped to the floor and a purple halo illuminated him. He was preparing to do his special attack!

And then . . .

Lance Slashblade curled up into a tight little ball and rolled at the jar, feebly tapping into it again and again like a helpless hedgehog.

"Ugh!" he grunted pathetically with each tap. "Ugh!"

"Oh, boy," Anger said.

"Psst," Joy whispered to Riley's Deep Dark Secret. "A little help?"

Deep Dark Secret grumbled and struck the jar with a massive hand. The glass shattered in one blow.

"Great job, Dark Secret!" Bloofy praised him as the Emotions stepped out, free. "Now it's your turn to help us! My fanny pack has just the thing to get us out of here. Everybody say, 'Oh, Pouchy!' "

The Emotions looked at one another and shrugged. "Oh, Pouchy!"

In a burst of green sparkles, the fanny pack around Bloofy's waist unbuckled and spiraled into the air, revealing two round cartoon eyes and a huge zipper grin.

"Hi, everybody!" the fanny pack said in a squeaky voice. "I'm Pouchy!"

"Pouchy, we need to escape," Bloofy explained. "Do you have anything that can help us?"

"I have lots of items!" Pouchy chirped. "Which one do you think will work the best?"

Items magically began appearing beside Pouchy in the air.

"A tomato?" Pouchy squeaked as a red tomato popped into existence. "A frog? Or exploding dynamite?"

"Oh, for crying out loud." Anger grabbed the dynamite, lit the top with his flaming head, and threw it toward the safe door.

KA-BOOM!

The safe blasted open, freeing the Emotions and Riley's secrets.

"We did it, everyone!" Bloofy cheered. "Let's all sing the 'We Did It' song!" Bloofy took a deep breath.

"No time!" Joy said, stopping him. They needed to save Riley.

"Thank you, friends." Lance Slashblade swept into a deep, dramatic bow. "I must be leaving you."

"What about Dark Secret?" Sadness looked over Lance's shoulder at Riley's Deep Dark Secret, who lingered inside the busted safe.

Deep Dark Secret picked up the safe door from

the ground. "Not yeeeeeeeeet." His voice faded as he slowly fit the door back into place, sealing himself inside.

"Yeah, that's probably best for everybody," Joy said.

Suddenly, a police whistle shrieked behind them.

"Hey!" shouted one of the Mind cops they'd seen before. He was now holding a steaming cup of coffee and a donut. "Who let you out? Get back in there!"

The Emotions gasped as a line of Mind cops sprinted around the corner and headed straight toward them.

"Oh, no!" Fear exclaimed.

"What are we going to do?" Disgust groaned.

Beside her, Lance Slashblade looked down at the small green Emotion, and his eyes burned with determination. He knelt in front of her.

"Oh, Disgusted One, as you once believed in me, I will now believe in myself."

Dropping his sword to the ground, Lance Slashblade curled into a ball once more.

The Mind cops stopped, weirded out.

"What—what's he doing?" one asked nervously.

Lance began a slow roll toward the cops. He missed them all, but he knocked into a mop as he passed by. It hit a cop on the head. That cop bumped into a second cop, who caused a third cop to spill his coffee, which made a fourth slip and fall into an open safe door. All the while, Lance continued rolling forward, not hitting a single Mind cop, but somehow causing each and every one to incapacitate themselves until they all accidentally locked themselves in a vault.

"Whaaa?" Sadness said in disbelief.

"Heh, heh, yeah!" Anger fist-pumped approvingly. "I love a good slapstick routine!"

"Oh, Lance." Disgust swooned.

Lance Slashblade rolled to the end of the hall. "Goodbye, friends!" His voice echoed as he rolled around a corner, vanishing from sight. "Hello, destiny!"

"Well, there's a lid for every pot," Joy said. Then she turned to the others. "Come on! We have to save Riley!"

Chapter 15

Headquarters was dark. Ennui lay snoring on the couch, her long purple arms draped lazily over the armrest, while Envy was curled up at her feet, snuggled under a blanket. Anxiety slept awkwardly in an office-style rolling chair, her head repeatedly lolling to one side before she straightened it up in her sleep, only for it to loll to the side once again in her restless slumber. Even in sleep, Anxiety vibrated.

Eventually the new Emotions would have their own beds, just like the core Emotions did. But Headquarters was still undergoing its overhaul, and in all the commotion, things like beds had taken a back burner. For now, sofas and rolling chairs would have to do.

At least it was peaceful. Riley was a sound sleeper, and thanks to her exhaustion from Coach Roberts's intense training session, she was deep in a dreamless sleep cycle.

Occasionally, Ennui's phone would buzz with a console update alert. But otherwise, Headquarters was quiet.

That is, it was until the emergency phone rang. Anxiety jerked awake, the pupils of her buggy eyes dilated in the darkness. She shook the cobwebs of sleep away. Ennui and Envy must have been sound asleep, because they didn't even stir. Anxiety picked up the phone.

"Uh, Headquarters," a Mind cop nervously said, "we have a situation."

"What is it?" Anxiety asked, her voice croaky.

"The, uh—the prisoners," the Mind cop said. "They, uh—they escaped."

All traces of grogginess drained from Anxiety as adrenaline kicked in. She vibrated with annoyance.

"I see," she said before hanging up. Then she turned her attention to the imageless projection screen, situated above the gently pulsing lights of the control console.

She had work to do.

"What do we do?" Fear exclaimed as the core Emotions raced down the stairs of the Vault. Even though they had busted out, it was only a matter of time before swarms of Mind cops would be on them again. How were they going to make it back?

"Those new Emotions have control of Riley!" Disgust gazed at Headquarters, which was slowly filling with orange light.

"Well, what are we waiting for?" Anger pounded a fist into his palm. "Let's go!"

"Whoa," Joy said, blocking Anger's path. "Where are you going?"

Anger was confused. "Back to Headquarters! To help Riley!"

"Riley's not up there," Joy said. "She's out *there*." She pointed toward the Back of the Mind, where they could see the tiny glowing dot of the Sense of Self on the horizon.

They'd been in tough spots before. They could do this. They just needed a plan, and plans started with first steps, and the first step was to get back their girl—the one Anxiety had banished to the Back of the Mind.

"We can't go back without her Sense of Self," Joy explained.

"You want us to go to the Back of the Mind?" Fear looked like his eyes were going to pop out. "Are you out of *your* mind?"

"But, Joy," said Sadness, "how will we get back if no one goes up to Headquarters?"

Just then, an alarm from the Vault went off, its blaring siren slicing through the moment of quiet. Their time was up. Joy began running in the opposite direction of Headquarters. Even though they still didn't understand the plan, the other Emotions followed.

"We need to get our Riley back before Anxiety makes a new one," Joy said.

"But how do we get there?" asked Disgust. "Do you even have a plan, Joy?"

"I bet Anxiety would have a really good plan," Fear said.

"A plan? Sure! Of course I do," Joy said, trying not to be offended by Disgust's and Fear's comments. "Anxiety's not the only one who can project the future. How hard could it be?"

The other Emotions looked at her doubtfully, but Joy pushed on. "First, all we have to do is . . . umm . . . follow the Stream of Consciousness!"

The Emotions nodded, picturing the river that flowed through Riley's mind, carrying all sorts of random memories and thoughts and objects.

"Then we take a nice, easy float all the way to the Back of the Mind!" Joy added.

"Oh! Where all the bad memories are!" Fear interjected. He remembered the few bad memories they had sent to the Back of the Mind using the tube.

"Exactly! And Riley's true Sense of Self!" Joy said. "We put her Sense of Self back. Then Riley will be Riley again." She imagined herself kneeling next to a crying Anxiety. "And then I tell Anxiety, 'Hey, don't worry so much anymore.' And she'll say, 'Wow, Joy, I never thought of that before! Thank you!' And then we hug and become best friends."

"And then I punt her into the dump," Anger added.

"What? No! Anger!" Joy admonished him.

"Okay, fine. No punting," Anger agreed.

"That's all great, Joy," said Sadness. "But how are we going to—"

"Get to the stream?" Joy interrupted. "Great question, Sadness! It's right over there!"

She led everyone to an area of Riley's mind called Long Term Memory, where long stacks of shelves, stretching as far as the eye could see, held countless memory spheres. Joy sprinted around the corner of a tall stack of memories, leading the Emotions . . . right into a dead end.

"Huh?" Joy said, confused. That hadn't been there the last time she and Sadness had been in Long Term Memory—at least not that Joy remembered. *Oh, no.*

"Uh, Joy? This is a dead end," Disgust pointed out super helpfully.

"Those are the worst kinds of ends!" Fear fretted.

"Everything is changing so fast." Sadness melted to the floor in an immovable pool of woe.

"So we're lost." Anger's flame smoldered.

"No!" Joy protested. "You're never lost if you're having . . . fun!"

Disgust gave her a condescending look as the police siren blared closer. "No one is having fun, Joy."

"Oh, come on." Joy gestured to Sadness, who was face down on the ground. "Look at Sadness! She's having a great time!"

"I thought you knew where you were going," Anger said.

"I do! I did—I just—*Ugh!*" Joy huffed in exasperation. Could these guys seriously be any more negative? It felt like she was the only one trying to keep things together. Didn't they get how hard she was trying? "I just need a moment . . ."

But Disgust rolled her eyes. "She doesn't know."

"We're stuck here!" Fear wailed.

Anger shook his fist in the air. "Curse you, puberty!"

Joy was about to say something—she didn't

know what, but something very, very authoritative to refute the Emotions' attitudes, because they were most definitely *not* stuck if only they could all look on the bright side for one single time in their lives—when, suddenly, the world lit up.

"Oh! Riley's awake!" Sadness picked up her head from the ground, where she was still collapsed in a puddle.

"Something's not right," Joy said. She had a bad feeling in the pit of her stomach. What was Anxiety doing to their girl? They couldn't afford more delays. "Come on! We'll find another way!"

As the Emotions dashed toward the glowing speck of the Sense of Self in the distance, Joy hoped with everything she had that their girl would hang on for just a while longer.

"Don't worry, Riley," Joy murmured. "We're coming."

EMBARRASSMENT·ENNUI·ENVY·FEAR·JOY·SADNESS·ANGER·ANXIETY·DISG
NESS·ANGER·ANXIETY·DISGUST·EMBARRASSMENT·ENNUI·ENVY·FEAR·JO
MBARRASSMENT·ENNUI·ENVY·FEAR·JOY·SADNESS·ANGER·ANXIETY·DISG
EAR·JOY·SADNESS·ANGER·ANXIETY·DISGUST·EMBARRASSMENT·ENNUI·E
NVY·FEAR·JOY·SADNESS·ANGER·ANXIETY·DISGUST·EMBARRASSMENT·EN
NXIETY·DISGUST·EMBARRASSMENT·ENNUI·ENVY·FEAR·JOY·SADNESS·AN
MENT·ENNUI·ENVY·FEAR·JOY·SADNESS·ANXIETY·DISGUST·EMBARRASSM
ETY·DISGUST·EMBARRASSMENT·ENNUI·ENVY·FEAR·JOY·SADNESS·ANGER
ENT·ENNUI·ENVY·FEAR·JOY·SADNESS·ANGER·ANXIETY·DISGUST·EMBARR
·ANGER·ANXIETY·DISGUST·EMBARRASSMENT·ENNUI·ENVY·FEAR·JOY·SA
RASSMENT·ENNUI·ENVY·FEAR·JOY·SADNESS·ANXIETY·DISGUST·EMBARR
SADNESS·ANGER·ANXIETY·DISGUST·EMBARRASSMENT·ENNUI·ENVY·FEAR
MBARRASSMENT·ENNUI·ENVY·FEAR·JOY·SADNESS·ANGER·ANXIETY·DISG
NESS·ANGER·ANXIETY·DISGUST·EMBARRASSMENT·ENNUI·ENVY·FEAR·JO
MBARRASSMENT·ENNUI·ENVY·FEAR·JOY·SADNESS·ANGER·ANXIETY·DISG
EAR·JOY·SADNESS·ANGER·ANXIETY·DISGUST·EMBARRASSMENT·ENNUI·E
NVY·FEAR·JOY·SADNESS·ANGER·ANXIETY·DISGUST·EMBARRASSMENT·E
NXIETY·DISGUST·EMBARRASSMENT·ENNUI·ENVY·FEAR·JOY·SADNESS·AN
MENT·ENNUI·ENVY·FEAR·JOY·SADNESS·ANXIETY·DISGUST·EMBARRASSM
ETY·DISGUST·EMBARRASSMENT·ENNUI·ENVY·FEAR·JOY·SADNESS·ANGER
ENT·ENNUI·ENVY·FEAR·JOY·SADNESS·ANGER·ANXIETY·DISGUST·EMBARR
·ANGER·ANXIETY·DISGUST·EMBARRASSMENT·ENNUI·ENVY·FEAR·JOY·SA
RASSMENT·ENNUI·ENVY·FEAR·JOY·SADNESS·ANXIETY·DISGUST·EMBARRA
SADNESS·ANGER·ANXIETY·DISGUST·EMBARRASSMENT·ENNUI·ENVY·FEAR
MBARRASSMENT·ENNUI·ENVY·FEAR·JOY·SADNESS·ANGER·ANXIETY·DISG
NESS·ANGER·ANXIETY·DISGUST·EMBARRASSMENT·ENNUI·ENVY·FEAR·JO
MBARRASSMENT·ENNUI·ENVY·FEAR·JOY·SADNESS·ANGER·ANXIETY·DISG
EAR·JOY·SADNESS·ANGER·ANXIETY·DISGUST·EMBARRASSMENT·ENNUI
NVY·FEAR·JOY·SADNESS·ANGER·ANXIETY·DISGUST·EMBARRASSMENT·E
NXIETY·DISGUST·EMBARRASSMENT·ENNUI·ENVY·FEAR·JOY·SADNESS·AN
MENT·ENNUI·ENVY·FEAR·JOY·SADNESS·ANXIETY·DISGUST·EMBARRASSM
ETY·DISGUST·EMBARRASSMENT·ENNUI·ENVY·FEAR·JOY·SADNESS·ANGER
ENT·ENNUI·ENVY·FEAR·JOY·SADNESS·ANGER·ANXIETY·DISGUST·EMBARR
·ANGER·ANXIETY·DISGUST·EMBARRASSMENT·ENNUI·ENVY·FEAR·JOY·SA
RASSMENT·ENNUI·ENVY·FEAR·JOY·SADNESS·ANXIETY·DISGUST·EMBARR

Chapter 16

The chill air stung Riley's cheeks as she skated around the empty rink. The sun hadn't even risen yet, and the sound of her skates slicing across the ice was the only noise in the deserted arena. Her muscles were still sore from the previous day's training, and they ached in protest as she warmed up, but this was the only way, she thought. She needed extra time on the ice. She needed to get better. Normally Riley was a sound sleeper, but that morning she'd woken up at four in her dorm room, thinking about what Grace and Bree had said, and she hadn't been able to stop their words from rattling around in her head.

It's nearly impossible to get on varsity as a freshman.

Let's be real.

Riley *was* being real. Two days earlier it hadn't mattered as much if she made varsity in her freshman year. But now it did, because she wanted—no, needed—this chance to turn things around. To make them right. To go into high school knowing that a whole team of friends would have her back—that she wouldn't be alone.

I need to play better than ever, Riley thought, gathering a cart of hockey pucks and preparing to run an Iron Cross drill. *I need to prove I can do it. I need to make the team. Or else . . .*

She didn't want to think about the alternative.

Ennui groaned as she sat up from the couch, her lanky body stiff and awkwardly twisted. She stretched and blinked. Envy was no longer curled up at her feet. Instead, the little teal Emotion's blanket was discarded in a heap on the floor and she was standing across the room beside Anxiety, who was scribbling furiously at her whiteboard. The screen was on, and it was bright in HQ despite Ennui's phone saying it was still five in the morning.

"Okay, team. Let's get going," said Anxiety.

"Why did we wake up Riley so early?" Ennui groaned.

"Joy got out," Anxiety said shortly. "So we need to

speed things up." She turned and flashed Ennui a twitchy smile. "Pop quiz! We're here so Riley has what next year?"

Envy raised her hand like an eager student. "What everyone else has!"

"Close," Anxiety said, pointing her dry-erase marker at Envy.

"Detached discontent?" Ennui quipped.

"No!" Anxiety said.

Embarrassment lumbered over to them. There hadn't been a couch or a chair big enough for him to sleep on the previous night, so he'd slept on the floor. The large pink Emotion whispered something in Anxiety's ear.

"That's right!" Anxiety said. "Friends!" She flipped her whiteboard over and wrote the word in huge capital letters. "We *need* her to be a Fire Hawk so she has *friends*. That means we hit the ice early and we practice like we've never practiced before!"

Everyone turned to watch Riley running an Iron Cross drill on the ice. Her skates moved in perfect rhythm as she expertly swiveled the puck back and forth with her hockey stick.

"Aren't we already good at hockey?" Envy asked.

"We are, but we need to be great!" Anxiety insisted.

Riley shot the puck at the goal and missed.

"Every time we miss, we skate a lap around the rink." Anxiety pressed a button on the console.

Disappointed in herself, Riley grunted in frustration and skated a lap. Then she repeated the drill and lined up another shot. She missed.

"Hockey is not a game. It's a sport!" Anxiety proclaimed as Riley skated another lap.

Riley took shot after shot and skated lap after lap until, finally, she scored a goal.

"Wow! That was amazing!" Envy breathed.

"But we could be better!" Anxiety's face glowed in the light of the screen. "Let's run it again!"

On the ice, Riley reveled in her perfect shot for the briefest of moments before thinking about the previous thirty she'd missed.

Come on, Andersen, she thought bitterly. *Step it up. You should be making every single one of these shots. You're better than this.*

Grace's words floated through her head.

Let's be real.

"Oh, I'm real," Riley said to herself. "And I'm good. I just need to make sure that they see it every single time." She took a deep breath. She was going to practice this drill all morning if she had to. What time was it, anyway?

Riley turned to see if there was a clock on the arena wall, and she gasped.

She wasn't alone. Val was standing at the entrance to the rink.

"Aye!" Val waved and smiled. "I see I'm not the only one who likes to start early."

"You guys!" Anxiety smacked the other Emotions' shoulders enthusiastically. "It's Val! We had the same idea!"

"We're basically the same person!" Envy squealed. "We're going to be best friends!"

As Val skated up to Riley on the rink, she glanced at the net and noticed the number of pucks piled up around it. "Uh . . . how long have you been here?"

Embarrassment gently touched a button on the console, and Riley rubbed the back of her neck, her cheeks flushing pink. "I don't know," she said. "Maybe an hour? I just wanted to get in some extra ice time."

Luckily, Val didn't seem to think Riley's answer was weird. In fact, she smiled. "I'm the same way."

"Oh my gosh, she gets us!" Anxiety exclaimed.

Val put an arm around Riley's shoulder like a big sister. "See? I told the other girls you'd figure it out. You get what it takes to be the best."

In HQ, a tinkling sound emanated as a new orange memory sphere rolled out. Anxiety hummed with excitement as she rushed to collect it. Inside the shimmering sphere was an image of Val saying "what it takes to be the best."

"This is going great!" Envy cheered.

"Yup!" Anxiety agreed. "But we need Val to really like us."

"We should ask Val lots of questions!" Envy suggested. "People love talking about themselves!"

"So, what was freshman year on the Fire Hawks like?" Riley asked, shooting another puck into the goal.

"I mean, it was a lot of work," Val admitted. "But it's also how I met my best friends."

Anxiety could scarcely believe how well this was going. "Val is *sharing* things with us!"

"Hey." Val stopped like an idea had struck her. "A few

of us are just going to hang out tonight, order some food. You should come."

"Ooh," Envy cooed. "An exclusive invitation. We're going!"

"Really?" Riley asked Val, her voice filled with hope.

"Definitely." Val nodded. "It'll be fun."

Just then, all the remaining hockey players arrived, chatting and ready to hit the ice for practice. Some held half-eaten bagels in their hands, while others were still stretching and yawning. Val noticed Bree and Grace as they waved at Riley.

"You should bring your friends," Val said.

"Sure." Riley smiled, though her voice was a little tight.

"We are *not* sharing Val with them!" Envy's eyes flashed.

Val and Riley skated toward the rest of their team.

"Early mornings make me so hungry!" Val said.

"I know, right?" Riley replied. "I'd give *anything* for a piece of pizza right now."

"Yes!" Val agreed.

"One more thing we have in common with Val!" Envy cheered. "Does this make us best friends yet?"

Anxiety hurried to the memory wall and gathered an

armful of orange spheres. "Envy, you're in the zone. Take the wheel. I'll be back."

Envy looked like she might launch into the air as she bounced up and down with excitement. "She picked me!" Envy squeaked. "Did you see that, Ennui? She picked me!"

Ennui rolled her eyes. "You care too much about things."

While Envy managed the console, Anxiety scurried to the Belief System elevator doors with her armful of orange memories. She took the long ride down.

After exiting the elevator, Anxiety strode to the stream and dropped the pile of orange memories into it, causing the water to ripple and radiate with an orange glow. New belief strings began to grow, stretching up, tall and strong.

Anxiety plucked a string, and Riley's voice echoed.

If I'm good at hockey, I'll have friends.

Anxiety exhaled in relief. "If we just stick to my plan, everything will be all right."

Chapter 17

"See! I told you I'd find it! The Stream of Consciousness!"

Joy panted as she and the other core Emotions came upon a wide river flowing with objects inspired by Riley's thoughts. Because Riley was thinking about food, the stream was full of her favorites. Joy followed its path with her gaze, watching as it flowed steadily deeper into Riley's mind. This waterway was their ticket to the Back of the Mind, where, they hoped, Riley's true Sense of Self was still intact. Joy cringed when she remembered the way Anxiety had ripped it from its pedestal. And now Anxiety's beliefs were growing like weeds, overtaking and weakening every belief strand Joy and the other core Emotions had worked so hard to help Riley build. Joy had to keep reminding herself that their girl was strong; Riley wouldn't let her old Sense of Self die away—not that easily.

Fear noticed all the food in the stream. “Whoa! Our girl is hungry!”

“Come on! Hop on something delicious!” Joy said. She noticed a slice of pizza floating past and grabbed it.

Disgust, Fear, and Anger took a seat on the pillowy crust.

“Ooh, deep dish,” said Disgust. “That’s nice.”

“And it’s still warm!” Fear added, settling into the bubbly cheese.

“First class all the way!” Joy cheered.

Before Joy hopped onto the pizza boat, Sadness stopped her. “But I’ve been trying to tell you. We can’t take the tube back. Someone has to be at the console to recall us.”

“She’s right, Joy,” said Disgust. “We’d be stranded.”

Fear shook his head. “I bet Anxiety would’ve thought of that.”

Disgust, Fear, and Anger jumped off the pizza back to shore.

Joy sighed, frustrated that there was a massive flaw in her plan. She watched the pizza slice float downstream. Then she noticed a recall tube nearby. She pointed at it. “Well . . . then someone’s gonna have to crawl up that tube and go back to Headquarters and, at the right moment, recall us!"

Anger mashed his fists together. "Oh, I'll do it. I'll pound that orange—"

"I don't think so, punty," said Joy. Anger might mean business, but he might also forget his business of bringing them back while taking care of "punting" business.

"Then who?" Anger quietly smoldered.

They all looked at Fear.

"Ah . . . well, here's the thing . . ." Fear started nervously.

"You were never an option." Joy shook her head.

Fear sighed in relief. "Oh, good."

Next they looked at Disgust.

"Me, crawl through a tube?" Disgust pointed to herself indignantly. "In this? I don't think so."

Finally, they all stared at Sadness.

"Oh, no! Not me!" Sadness protested.

"Yes, Sadness! You could do it!" Joy insisted. "You know the console better than anybody! You've read the manuals cover to cover."

"I mean, you say that, but I know a lot less about Manual 28, Chapter 7, 'How to Recall Non-Memory Objects,' than most folks realize," Sadness pointed out.

Joy smiled. "You're provin' my point for me, Sadness! That sounds like a yes!"

She grabbed two walkie-talkies from a nearby pile of construction debris. They crackled to life when she hit the "on" switch. "We'll signal you when we've got Riley's Sense of Self. And then you bring us back!"

But Sadness trembled as Joy opened the hatch to the recall tube. The Mind cops' sirens grew louder.

"Ohhh . . ." Sadness groaned, looking like she would rather be anywhere in the world than there.

"Sadness, it's the fastest way back to Headquarters," Joy told her.

"Joy, I can't do it." Sadness shook her head vehemently. "I'm not strong like you are."

Joy locked eyes with her friend. "I know you, Sadness. You *are* strong. I can't give you specific examples right now, but you got this!" With effort, Joy heaved Sadness up inside the tube.

Reluctantly, Sadness wiggled into the tube and began the long climb back to Headquarters. "Oh, yeah, I can do it . . ." she said, sobbing, as Joy closed the hatch.

"She'll be okay, right?" Joy asked Anger.

"Eh, fifty-fifty," Anger replied.

After more intense drills with the team, Riley took a water break with Val. Riley's stomach emitted a loud gurgle. Her eyes darted to Val.

"What was *that*?" Anxiety exclaimed.

"All that thinking about food made us hungry!" said Envy.

Val offered her protein bar to Riley. "Want a bite?"

"We hate those things!" Envy whined. "They taste like cardboard."

Anxiety gasped. "We can't say no to Val!"

"Okay, no, you're so right," Envy said. "We eat whatever Val eats!"

"Uh, sure," Riley said hesitantly. She took a bite, trying to hide a grimace.

Val smiled. "Tastes great, right?"

"Mmm," Riley said. "It's got a very interesting texture. It tastes like . . . What does it remind me of?"

Joy, Anger, Fear, and Disgust returned to the Stream of Consciousness.

"Okay, everyone. Jump on the next cheesy, melt-in-your-mouth slice of pizza you see," Joy said.

But Joy quickly realized Riley's thoughts had changed. She gasped. "Cardboard? Asparagus? Broccoli? What are they doing to her up there?"

Anger grabbed a giant broccoli floret. "I don't know, but we have to go."

"No! No way am I stepping one foot on that," Disgust insisted.

"We have to!" Anger exclaimed. "Riley needs us!"

Disgust groaned. Reluctantly, she stepped onto the squishy broccoli. "Ew! Ew! Ew!"

Fear and Joy jumped on next. The broccoli boat wobbled and spun in the stream's current.

"To the Back of the Mind!" Anger exclaimed.

Disgust gagged. "I think I'm going to be sick!"

Joy hadn't imagined sailing down the Stream of Consciousness on a broccoli floret. But as it swept them away to destinations unknown, she hoped it was taking them to the Riley they desperately needed to save.

Chapter 18

Riley breathed hard, her skates practically moving on their own as she powered forward on the ice, all her attention laser-focused on Val, who was maneuvering the puck along the left side of the rink. Riley was dead center, facing off against Bree, who stood goalie for Team Two.

Val snapped the puck to Riley, who lifted her hockey stick and walloped the puck straight past Bree's outstretched goalie glove and into the net.

"Okay, Miss Riley!" Val cheered.

"Nice one, Michigan!" Dani called from across the ice.

Riley lifted her face mask and grinned at them both. From the corner of her eye, she saw Bree shaking her head, frustrated that she'd let the puck get by.

"All right, ladies!" Coach Roberts blew her whistle. She jotted something down in a red notebook she'd been holding throughout camp and then nodded approvingly at the players. "Great day today. Take it easy tonight."

Riley exhaled, relaxing her aching shoulder muscles. She'd made it through day two. And more important, she'd made it to that night—her first time hanging out with the Fire Hawks! It was her chance to show them the true Riley—the Riley they could joke around with and have fun with and maybe one day even take selfies with, the same way she used to take selfies with . . .

She glanced at Bree and Grace, who were exiting the rink. She hadn't invited them to hang out, like Val had offered. But it wasn't Riley's job to make sure Bree and Grace knew *every* single detail about what was going on at camp, right? They could figure things out on their own, like Riley had been doing.

After changing back into her normal clothes, Riley joined the Fire Hawks outside the locker room.

"Hey, Michigan, how you holding up?" one of the girls asked as they all started walking.

"Oh, uh, pretty good, I guess," Riley said, suddenly aware that everyone's eyes had shifted to her. "I'm a little sore." Why was just talking making her heart pound?

"Yeah, Coach can be tough," another girl chimed in. "But you get used to it."

"Speaking of . . ." Dani pointed toward Coach

Roberts's office, which was a small room she'd been borrowing from the main college coach during the skills camp. Coach Roberts wasn't inside. She must have already left for the evening. However, her red notebook lay in the center of the desk.

"There it is," Dani said in an ominous tone to Riley. "The red notebook."

Val rolled her eyes. "Don't say it like that. You'll freak her out."

Confused, Riley looked at them. "Why would it freak me out?" Lots of coaches had notebooks, didn't they? To write down plays and stuff?

"Everything Coach thinks about you is in there," Dani said. "The good *and* the bad. Whether she wants you on the team . . ."

"Or not," another Fire Hawk, named Sofia, added in a serious tone right beside Riley, causing her to shiver.

Some of the girls chuckled in good fun, but Val huffed. "You guys! Too much."

"What?" Sofia shrugged. "It's the truth. She's going to find out sooner or later."

"Come on. I'm starving." Val moved them along. "Whatever Coach Roberts has written in there, we'll never know anyway, right?"

The Fire Hawks continued down the hall, but Riley stayed back for a moment, staring at the notebook.

Coach had written something in there after Riley had scored the goal on Bree.

Could everything Riley needed to know really be sitting right there in one little red notebook?

"What do you think she's written about us?" Envy's eyes were wide as she studied the notebook on the screen inside Headquarters.

"I don't know!" Anxiety exclaimed. "Do you think it's bad?"

"What if she's made a list of all her favorite players and we're not on it?" Envy wondered.

"Or a list of all the worst players and we're at the top," Anxiety added.

"Or worse," said Envy, "we're not on either list, and we fade into obscurity!"

Anxiety felt her panic rising. "What if she wrote down flaws in our game that we didn't even know existed?"

Envy gasped. "What if she drew a caricature of our face just because she can?"

"Um, they are walking away," Ennui interrupted.

Riley pushed away her worries and caught up to the Fire Hawks. She walked with them through the tall redwoods on the way to the dormitory common area. Everyone was chatting and enjoying themselves, but Riley couldn't figure out what to say. Never mind that: she couldn't even figure out how to walk normally.

"Uh, why do our arms swing like this when we walk?" Anxiety vibrated as she noted that not a single other girl's arms were swinging the way Riley's were.

"Try to keep them still," Envy suggested.

Anxiety pressed a button on the console, and Riley's arms went stiff at her sides.

"That's *more* weird!" Anxiety cried.

"Well, that wasn't my intention," Envy huffed. "I'm sorry for trying something!"

From her lounging position on the couch, Ennui sighed heavily. "What did you think pockets were for?" She tapped an icon on her console app, and Riley immediately shoved her hands into her pockets.

"Oh, Ennui. I am very proud of you," Anxiety said appreciatively.

Someone told a joke up ahead, and everyone laughed—except Riley.

"What are they laughing about?" Envy asked urgently. "Does anyone know what cool people laugh about?"

"I don't know." Anxiety shook. "We were too focused on the arms thing. Just pretend like we got the joke!"

A bit too forcefully, Anxiety pushed a console lever forward, and Riley let out an awkwardly loud laugh. Some of the Fire Hawks turned to give her an odd look.

Embarrassment face-palmed and hit the console, flooding it with pink.

Riley's cheeks flushed, and her laugh petered out as the Fire Hawks turned away.

Frustrated, Anxiety vibrated and tugged at her hair.

They just needed to play it cool. How hard was it to play it cool?

Chapter 19

In the depths of Riley's mind, the core Emotions continued their journey along the Stream of Consciousness. The river stretched on endlessly, and the Emotions struggled to balance on their very unstable broccoli boat. It didn't help that random objects bonked into them, threatening to topple them over. Anger, Fear, and Disgust bickered endlessly.

"Quit moving around!"

"You're making it worse!"

"I'm not moving. *You're* moving!"

"No, move left!"

"Get off me!"

"You're going to tip us!"

"I don't like this vessel," Fear whined.

"Well, that's all we have," Joy, unfazed, told him.

"How much longer until we get there?" Anger asked.

"We'll get there when we get there," Joy answered, remembering a phrase Riley's dad said often on long car trips.

"I bet Anxiety would know how long," said Fear. "Down to the minute."

Joy gritted her teeth, refusing to take the bait. "Well, she just knows everything, doesn't she?"

"Look, I don't like her words," Fear clarified. "I don't like her actions. I just—I think I could change her."

"You know what?" Joy said, her frustration uncharacteristically threatening to bubble over. Then she looked at each one of them before taking a deep breath and pushing her frustration down even deeper than before.

"Who likes banana bread?" she exclaimed with a forced smile. "Show of hands!"

The dormitory common area reminded Riley of a large but cozy ski lodge as the Fire Hawks spread out on the various couches and armchairs. The ceiling's wooden beams were hewn from richly stained redwood, and there was even a stone fireplace. A few study tables were nestled along the walls with little reading lamps, and a vending machine by the exit to the dorm rooms offered the promise of soda and candy (though, unfortunately, the only item in stock was water). In the center of the room was a foosball table, where some of the Fire Hawks were playing a game.

Riley was glad that the Fire Hawks had ordered pizza for dinner. She'd even managed to nab a garlic breadstick before they were all gone. But her first big hang with the group was proving awkward. Riley wished she had something to contribute to their conversations, but it seemed almost like they were speaking a different language, with their talk of driver's permits and social media scandals and advanced course selections. Every now and again someone mentioned one of the skills camp drills, and Riley nodded enthusiastically, ready to chime in. But just as swiftly, the topic shifted, and Riley swallowed the breath she'd taken to speak. She couldn't help feeling like a third wheel.

Then someone turned on a song that Riley had never heard before.

"Aw, heck yes!" Val exclaimed. "I love this song."

"Yeah, this is going on my birthday playlist," Dani replied.

"Oh, will you share that with me?" Val asked. "I still listen to the one you made last year."

A girl named Ally turned to Riley. "Who's your favorite band, Michigan?"

Riley exhaled in relief. This was an easy question. "Oh, Get Up and Glow!" she answered confidently. "They're awesome!"

"Get Up and Glow!" Val exclaimed. "I was all over them in middle school."

Dani scoffed. "Are you serious?"

"Yeah, I was a Glow Girlie," Val said with a laugh.

Riley gasped. What had she done?

"In middle school?" Anxiety said. "As in, when Val was a little kid? Does Val think *we're* a little kid? Do they *all* think we're a little kid?"

Embarrassment went to drive, but it was too much. He fainted.

"We need a band they think is cool. Not one we actually like!" said Anxiety.

"We need to recall everything we know about music!" Envy added.

Anxiety urgently hit a flashing recall button on the console.

Unbeknownst to Anxiety, deep within the recall tube, Sadness continued her long crawl back to Headquarters. Her sobs had dried out, mainly because she had to maintain her energy for the trek. If only there were a way to speed things along. But there wasn't a magical propulsion system within the tube unless someone recalled a memory from that specific passageway. And that was a one-in-a-million chance. So along Sadness crept, alone with her thoughts in the cramped, empty tube . . .

Suddenly, a rumbling sounded somewhere behind her. Sadness turned just in time to see a slew of memory spheres hurtling toward her as the recall tube suction sprang to life.

"Uh-oh . . ." she said.

In Headquarters, Anxiety watched impatiently as a massive pile of memory spheres burst out onto the floor. There must have been some punk rock in there somewhere, because she could have sworn she heard a scream as the spheres arrived. One memory dropped into Riley's recall projector. Anxiety hoped it was a good band. They all listened closely to hear what Riley had recalled.

The TripleDent Gum jingle echoed throughout HQ.

"Ugh! Get that out of there!" Anxiety cried.

Embarrassment (who had woken up from fainting) and Envy turned back to the pile and hurried to search for a better song. Embarrassment seemed a little distracted for some reason, probably because he was still discombobulated. But Envy was on the case, tossing sphere after sphere to the side.

"Keep searching!" Anxiety demanded. "Our future depends on a better answer!"

"That's the best we have!" Envy groaned. "These are mostly jingles and Dad's yacht rock."

Dani's voice emanated from the screen. "You don't still like them, do you?" She was looking right at Riley.

"What do we do?" Anxiety panicked. "If we don't like their music, we have nothing to offer these girls. We'll be outed as the imposter we so obviously are."

With a deep, dramatic sigh, Ennui finally stirred from her lounging position on the couch. She stretched and cracked her knuckles. "Pardon. *Excusez-moi.* I've been waiting my whole life for this very moment."

Anxiety, vibrating with terrified nerves, watched as Ennui sauntered over and pressed a single console button.

"Oh, yeah, I *loooooove* Get Up and Glow," Riley said, her voice dripping with sarcasm. She wasn't sure how the idea had come to her; it was almost like she was being sarcastic by instinct. But miraculously, a couple of the Fire Hawks chuckled, and Riley grinned. It had worked! She'd covered up her mistake.

"Oh, yeah, Get Up and Glow is *soooo* awesome," she said, overly dramatic again.

The Fire Hawks laughed now, enjoying the joke. Even Val seemed to get that Riley had just been messing around about liking Get Up and Glow, even though, well, Riley *did* like them. But there was no way she would ever admit to that again. No way, nohow.

"Riley, what are you talking about?"

Bree's voice startled Riley from across the room. Riley turned to see Bree and Grace arriving, carrying sandwiches from the college cafeteria.

Bree stared at Riley in surprise. "You love Get Up and Glow."

"My mom literally just took us to their concert," Grace added. She sounded more annoyed than surprised.

Riley felt her heart race again. She was caught in a lie. *Hockey sticks!* Why had Bree and Grace come in right then?

"Well, yeah. I mean, sure, but—"

"But what?" Grace pressed her. "We had a great time."

Riley eyed the Fire Hawks. They were all watching her. Every single one of them was watching her.

So she did the only thing she could think of to save face.

"Yeah, we had a *greaaat* time." Riley dramatically slipped back into her sarcastic tone.

The Fire Hawks laughed again at Riley's performance. And Riley leaned into the moment.

"Yeah, best night of my *liiiiife*."

Now some of the Fire Hawks had tears from laughing so hard. *This is working,* Riley thought. *They like my jokes!*

But Bree and Grace didn't look amused. Not at all.

"Well, this has been hilarious," Grace said curtly.

"But we're gonna go," Bree finished.

They each shot Riley an icy look before turning to leave.

"Ennui, that was inspired!" Anxiety bubbled in Headquarters. "Masterwork!"

Ennui polished her phone on her shirt and returned to the couch. “I know.”

A memory sphere rolled out, replaying the memory of the Fire Hawks laughing at Riley’s jokes. “See?” Anxiety chirped. “As long as we like what they like, we’ve got all the friends we need!”

Bree’s and Grace’s annoyed expressions hadn’t escaped Anxiety’s notice. She had never before seen them give Riley that look, almost as if they didn’t even like her. Maybe the Emotions had overdone the sarcasm. Anxiety hadn’t meant to make Bree and Grace so mad. Should Riley apologize?

Anxiety eyed the Fire Hawks on the screen. She couldn’t lose focus.

“They’re our future,” she murmured. “As long as we do everything we need to do to make them like us, we’ll be okay.”

Chapter 20

Anxiety and the other new Emotions had no idea that Riley's sarcasm had reverberated across the Mind World.

"I think we're almost there," Joy promised the others. The Stream of Consciousness current was moving faster now, and Joy watched as they passed half-constructed structures on either bank of the river. The Mind Workers were busy back in that part of Riley's mind, though what they were building wasn't exactly clear. Everything looked rather abstract and unfinished—like half-formed thoughts.

Joy wasn't actually sure how much farther they needed to go, but she needed to be a leader right then for Riley's sake, and that meant keeping everyone's spirits up. "I can almost see the Back of the Mind!"

Suddenly, Riley's voice echoed around them. It seemed to come from high above.

"Oh, yeah, I loooooove Get Up and Glow."

"Riley?" Joy whispered. What was going on?

The water rippled around them, and a low rumble shook their boat. Ahead, the ground split into a giant chasm, and water from the Stream of Consciousness spilled right through. They were headed straight for it!

"Ahhh!" screamed the Emotions.

"Abandon broccoli!" Joy shouted.

Everyone leapt for the nearest riverbank and grabbed hold of anything to keep themselves from floating over the colossal waterfall. Anger and Disgust held tight to Fear and made it to dry ground, but Joy was the last to jump, and she just missed the bank. With a cry, she grabbed the edge of the chasm and barely kept herself from dropping into the abyss.

"Joy!" Disgust shouted.

Joy watched as their broccoli boat plummeted over the edge, splashing down into the depths below. Even amid the chaos, Joy recognized that the multicolored splash pattern looked like the one in Riley's Belief System.

"Give us your hand!" Anger yelled as he, Disgust,

and Fear formed a chain to reach her. With adrenaline-fueled effort, they hoisted Joy to safety.

"Are you okay?" Disgust asked.

Joy nodded, barely able to speak because she was breathing so hard.

"What *is* that?" screamed Fear.

A nearby Mind Worker ran up to them. "That's a Sar-chasm. Riley's a teenager. This could open for miles! Run for your lives!" Then he dashed away.

"Sar-chasm?" Disgust repeated, confused.

Above, Riley's voice echoed again. *"Oh yeah, Get Up and Glow is my faaaaavorite band."*

"But she loves Get Up and Glow," Joy said, worried. "She has all their albums!"

"What's next, Anxiety?" Anger shouted toward Headquarters. "First our birth state, now our music! Is anything good enough for you?"

Fear began pacing in circles. "What now? If we can't follow the stream, we don't know where we're going! If we don't know where we're going, we can't follow the stream! It's an endless loop of tragedy and consequence!"

"Or we could just go ask those guys." Joy pointed to two Mind Workers operating a crane on the opposite side of the massive canyon.

"Oh, yeah, or that," Fear said.

Together, the Emotions waved wildly to get the Mind Workers' attention.

"Boy, are we lucky we ran into you guys!" Joy shouted.

"Please, we really need your help!" Fear cried.

"I bet you're the best crane crew in the world!" Disgust added, trying to butter them up.

On the other side of the Sar-chasm, the Mind Workers paused their crane when they heard the Emotions' shouts.

"Boy, are we *luckyyyyyyy* we ran into you guys!" Joy's voice echoed, but because of the Sar-chasm, its tone sounded super snarky.

"Huh?" One of the Mind Workers raised an eyebrow.

"We *reaaallllly* need your *helllp*," Fear called.

The Mind Worker looked at his companion. "What's their problem?"

Then came Disgust's voice. *"I bet you're the besssst crane crew in the worrrrld."*

The Mind Workers frowned. "Wow. Those guys are jerks."

"They're not even going to answer us?" Anger huffed, perturbed. "Wow. Those guys are jerks."

Riley's voice echoed again. *"Yeah, we had a greeeeeeat time."*

Another rumble erupted and the chasm widened.

"How are we going to get across if it keeps getting bigger?" Disgust asked.

"What would Anxiety do?" Anger wondered.

Fear nodded. "I think she'd probably build a bridge of some sort using found objects. She's so resourceful."

Joy took a breath and surveyed the situation. The truth was she didn't really have a clue how they were going to get to the Back of the Mind now. But the absolute worst thing they could do was stop, and if the others didn't have faith in her to lead them, that was exactly what was going to happen. Joy had to be the beacon of hope for everyone. She had to be the one to keep them going, for Riley's sake.

"Well, I can't do that," she admitted. "So we're just gonna have to walk around it! The long way—which is the best way!" When they all looked at her dubiously, she added, "A little exercise never hurt anyone."

"Are you sure about this?" Anger asked.

"Yep!" Joy said with a forced smile. "Stretch those hammies! Let's go!"

"Well, I'm gonna go to bed." Val stood up from her armchair in the common area and stretched.

"Oh, really?" Riley asked, a little bummed. Some of the Fire Hawks were starting another round of foosball, but Riley wasn't sure she should stick around if Val wasn't there.

"Yeah, it's late," Val said. "Plus you'll want to get some sleep before tomorrow's scrimmage."

Riley blinked. "What scrimmage?"

"It's just something Coach always does on the last day," Val explained.

"It's how Val made the team as a freshman," Dani added, spinning her foosball players to knock the ball into her opponent's goal.

"What? Don't tell her that," Val said, shooting Dani a look.

"Val scored two goals," Dani continued, scoring a foosball goal of her own for emphasis. "No freshman had ever done that."

"Dani, stop," Val warned her. Riley couldn't tell if Val was embarrassed by the accolades or if the scrimmage the next day was actually a really big deal.

"Technically, it's not your tryout for next year," Ally chimed in, grabbing a cold slice of pizza from one of the boxes. "But it basically is."

Yikes! There was no doubt now. The scrimmage *was* a big deal. Riley's mind started to race with a thousand questions.

Val must have seen that Riley was a little freaked out, because she put a hand on Riley's shoulder. "You'll do great. Just be yourself." Then she offered a fist bump.

"Did you hear that?" Anxiety hummed with nervous energy. "We could become a Fire Hawk tomorrow!"

Anxiety and the other Emotions in HQ couldn't believe it. They had less than twelve hours to transform Riley into the newer, better version of herself to impress Coach *and* the Fire Hawks.

"But how do we be ourself if our new self isn't ready yet?" Envy wondered. She glanced toward the empty pedestal.

Anxiety turned to the wall of orange memories that had rolled into HQ. "Then let's move these babies downstairs."

Together, Anxiety and Envy scooped up armfuls of

the orange memory spheres to carry down to the Belief System. Unseen by either of them, Sadness, who had toppled in with the overload of music memories earlier, spied them from her spot in a hidden corner.

"Poor Riley," Sadness whispered.

And unseen by Sadness, Embarrassment was watching *her*, his hood drawn so tightly it nearly covered his whole face. He'd spotted the little blue Emotion when she'd first come in with the recalled memories, but he hadn't said anything. He commiserated with Sadness; even though they'd met for only a short bit before, she seemed to get him. He had a feeling she really wanted what was best for Riley. He knew keeping her presence a secret would get him in trouble with Anxiety. And yet he had a feeling he should—at least for now.

Chapter 21

Days. It felt to the core Emotions like they had been traveling for days, trekking along the unending precipice of the Sar-chasm. In reality, it had been only a few hours. But their legs burned, their heads pounded, and each one of them was pretty sure they now knew how physically drained Riley felt after a week's worth of hockey practice. Yet finally, they reached the end of the Sar-chasm and were able to walk around to the other side.

"There! We did it!" Joy panted.

"My quads burn with the heat of a thousand suns," Fear said, collapsing dramatically.

"See? Exercise!" Joy said brightly even as her own muscles screamed in protest.

"I can't see Riley's Sense of Self anywhere!" Anger shouted.

Joy gazed at the reverse trek before them on the opposite side of the chasm. "Don't worry. We'll just double back the same distance we just walked."

"Uggghhh," the other Emotions groaned. But they followed Joy. They followed her straight into . . .

Bonk.

A wall. On the other side of the Sar-chasm was a wall blocking their return path.

"Oh! Good news!" Joy laughed a little hysterically. "There's a wall! But you know what they say: so what!"

Exhausted and without any other options, the Emotions followed Joy along the wall leading even deeper into Long Term Memory. Neither Joy nor Sadness had been that far into the depths of Riley's mind.

"We're getting deeper and deeper in, Joy," Anger said.

"Great observation!" Joy said cheerily. "Who wants to sing a song?"

"I know a song," Disgust replied. "It's called 'I Give Up.' "

Joy forced a smile so wide she looked like a bizarre mannequin. None of them got it, did they? None of them understood *how hard* she was working to simply keep it together and lead them to the Back of the Mind in a desperate attempt to save their girl.

"Or . . . let's play the quiet game!" Joy said a little too loudly. "One, two, three, *hush*."

Anger ignored her. "I haven't seen Riley's Sense of Self since we passed that new Procrastination Land."

"That place was weird," Disgust said. "The sign said 'Coming Soon,' but no one seemed to be working on it."

"What's 'procrastination' mean?" Fear asked.

Anger shrugged. "We'll look it up later."

As they reached another set of shelves, Joy spotted two Forgetters. They were Mind Workers who vacuumed up old memories that Riley didn't need to remember anymore.

"Excuse me," Joy said to the Forgetters. "Can you help us? We're—" She stopped as she noticed the memories they were vacuuming. "Wait, are you—Is that Bree and Grace? We can't forget about them."

One of the Forgetters, named Paula, barely even looked at Joy and the Emotions. "Sorry, the job's the job."

"And our job is to follow orders from Headquarters," said the other Forgetter, named Bobby.

"But those are Riley's best friends," said Joy.

"That's not what we heard," said Paula. She held up a paper called *The Rumor Mill* with the headline BREE AND GRACE GET UP AND GO . . . AWAY!

Joy was horrified.

"Now if you'll excuse us," said Bobby, "we've got a job to do." He aimed the vacuum at the shelf, but he and Paula suddenly stopped.

"Wait, what were we doing?" asked Paula.

"I don't remember," said Bobby.

Paula and Bobby eventually moved on to another shelf, completely forgetting their interaction with the Emotions.

Disgust sighed. "This is useless. Real Riley is out there somewhere, and we're never going to find her!"

"No, I can find her," Joy insisted. "I just need to get a better view."

Just then, she spotted a ray of hope—the one thing that could get them out of their impossible situation. It was a freestanding construction lift meant for carrying Mind Workers to the top of the tall Long Term stacks. And it was unattended, meaning anyone could ride it, like four rogue Emotions . . .

Desperately, she pressed the control buttons to bring

it to life. Aside from a few creaks and groans, nothing happened.

"Okay, well, this isn't working." Joy could feel one of her eyes twitching, like Anxiety's had the other day. Before they'd been kicked out of their home. Before everything had gone wrong. She swallowed hard, her mouth dry. "And that's fine," she said. "Everything's fine."

"Joy, face it," Anger said. "You don't know what you're doing."

"I know it seems like that now," Joy countered. "And also earlier. And also back in Headquarters, but—"

Disgust shook her head. "I say we cut our losses and walk back. This is hopeless."

"This whole trip is just a series of deader and deader ends," Fear agreed.

"Ever since that Puberty Alarm went off, nothing around here works the way it's supposed to," Anger added.

"I don't even recognize this place anymore." Disgust sighed. "It's light outside at one in the morning!"

"I have *never* been inside so many jars in my life!" cried Fear.

Joy could feel herself losing it. *Keep it together,* she mentally urged herself. *Keep. It. Together.*

"Riley's Sense of Self is lost," Disgust said. "We are never getting back to Headquarters."

"And if Joy can't see that," Anger said, "well, then, she's *delusional*."

That was the end of Joy's patience. One too many jabs, one too many protests, one too many moans and groans and whines and cries and *why was she the only one trying here*?

"Of course I'm delusional!" Joy exploded. "Do you know how *hard* it is to stay positive all the time? When all you folks do is complain, complain, complain? Jiminy mother-lovin' toaster strudel! Do you think I have all the answers? Of course I don't!"

Anger, Fear, and Disgust stared at her, taken aback. Joy was never that out of control.

"We can't even find the back of our own mind!" Joy shouted, flooding with frustration at the reality of those words.

Exhausted, Joy collapsed beside the defunct lift. In a weird way, it was a relief to finally express her pent-up desperation. But on the other hand, it made it that much more definite: this was a hopeless cause. The chances of finding Riley's old Sense of Self and getting it back to HQ in time were one in a million. Their poor, poor girl. What would happen to her?

"Anxiety is right. Riley doesn't need us as much as she needs them," Joy said sadly. "And that hurts. It really hurts."

Silence fell over the friends for a moment, with just the distant hammers of Mind Workers building something somewhere echoing around them.

"Joy," Anger began, "you've made a lot of mistakes. *A lot.* And you'll make a whole lot more in the future. But if you let that stop you, we might as well lie down and give up now."

Joy looked up at him.

"Well, actually, that does sound kind of nice," Fear mused.

Disgust flicked him on the nose.

"Ow! What?"

Joy smiled. Anger smiled in return and held out his hand. "Come on."

The reassurance in his voice made Joy feel like she was about to cry. She took his hand.

Anger nodded and then approached the Forgetters. "Excuse us," he said with authority. In one quick motion, he snatched the vacuum from their hands.

"Hey! You can't use that!" Paula exclaimed.

"Sure we can," said Anger.

"Yeah, you told us we could use this whenever we wanted," added Disgust.

"We did?" asked Bobby.

Disgust nodded. "You must have forgotten."

"Oh. Oh yeah," said Paula.

"That does sound like us," Bobby agreed.

Anger, Fear, and Disgust mounted the hose.

Anger turned to Joy. "Hop on."

Joy climbed aboard just before Anger flipped the vacuum switch to reverse.

Ploom! Dozens of memory spheres shot out, propelling the team into the air.

"Ahhhh!" shouted the Emotions.

With a thud, they landed on top of the Long Term stacks. They were a bit rattled but not much worse for wear.

"There it is!" Fear cried.

It was the Sense of Self!

Seeing the glowing beacon filled Joy with hope. She looked at her friends and felt a rush of gratitude as they each nodded in turn.

"Go ahead," Anger told her confidently. "We're right behind you."

CHAPTER 21

Riley sat on the bed in her dorm room, holding the Get Up and Glow limited edition jacket Bree and Grace had gotten her for her birthday. She didn't know why she'd even brought it to camp, since it was summer. But in the rush to shove everything into her suitcase the other morning, she'd rolled it up and stuffed it in, thinking maybe she might be chilly if they had downtime on the ice.

Riley cringed, remembering the way Bree and Grace had looked at her earlier. She really hadn't meant for them to overhear her making fun of Get Up and Glow. It wasn't anything against them at all, but she could tell from the looks on their faces that they had taken it that way. What a mess. Maybe she should go talk to them.

And . . . tell them what? That she was pretending to like the stuff the Fire Hawks liked so they would like her? That sounded pathetic, even though Riley knew it was *exactly* what she was doing. But it wasn't like she had time to get to know them the way she'd gotten to know Bree and Grace over the past year. Things were complicated now. Riley had to build a new team around herself, and for what it was worth, the Fire Hawks seemed really nice.

That Ally girl had even mentioned Riley could be playing with them the next year, which meant they believed in her! More than Bree and Grace did, anyway.

She thought about the pizza party they'd just had and how she'd cheered on Dani in her final foosball match and how the girls had all waved good night before heading off to their dorms, like . . . friends.

Bree and Grace knew Riley better than anyone else in the world. They knew what her favorite soda was and that she had a fear of snakes, and they knew about that one time when she laughed so hard that her sports drink spewed out of her nose. But Riley liked being with the Fire Hawks, too. Hanging out with them made her feel like a winner. Her dad said she would knock the coach's skates off. With the Fire Hawks, she could do that.

"Ugh." Riley balled up the jacket and tossed it back into her suitcase. She didn't want to think about all that stuff right then. It was too confusing. Instead, she leaned back on her pillow and closed her eyes, images of laughing with the Fire Hawks over pizza replaying in her mind. That was a good memory—one worth dreaming about.

"This is great." Anxiety rubbed her hands together. "The Fire Hawks have accepted us. *But* if Coach doesn't put us on the team, none of that matters." She looked at the screen—Riley was just beginning to drift off—and she began pressing buttons on the console.

"Tomorrow is everything," Envy agreed.

"Which is why we're going to need more help!" Anxiety declared. She glanced at Ennui, who lazily tapped away at her phone.

"Ennui, are you paying attention?" Anxiety snapped.

"Non," Ennui replied without looking up.

Anxiety rolled her eyes and turned to Embarrassment. "Embarrassment? How about you?"

Embarrassment didn't respond. He was preoccupied with watching some memory from the memory wall.

"Embarrassment? Hello?" Anxiety said. Then she let out a disgruntled sigh. "Ugh, never mind."

Embarrassment had heard Anxiety talking to him. But he couldn't pull his eyes away from the memory sphere he held in his hands. It showed the moment Bree and Grace had given Riley the icy look and walked away.

"Well, this has been hilarious."

"But we're gonna go."

Embarrassment hugged his hoodie a little tighter around himself. He wasn't sure how to feel about the memory. Riley had saved herself from being embarrassed in front of the Fire Hawks. But meanwhile, she'd done something worse. She'd felt ashamed in front of Bree and Grace. Anxiety might not see it that way. But he did.

He was about to walk over to the console when he heard a soft clunk in the construction debris behind him. Curious, he peeked under a demolished I beam. He gasped.

Sadness was hiding right there! She crouched, frozen, realizing she'd been caught.

Embarrassment looked at the other Emotions and then back at Sadness. None of them had spotted her.

Sadness gazed up at him with wide, watery eyes. "Shhh," she whispered.

She was trusting him. Why was she trusting him? Perhaps for the same reason he hadn't sounded the alarm when he saw her sneak in. He couldn't help feeling like he and Sadness understood each other.

Embarrassment reached out, and Sadness shrank back, probably thinking he was going to nab her. Then he shifted a pile of books in front of her so she was fully hidden. Sadness peeked out and smiled before ducking down behind the books. And under his hoodie, Embarrassment smiled, too.

Meanwhile, Anxiety was furiously at work over the console. She popped up her projection laptop, and it glowed to life. "All right, guys, it's going to be a long night." She chugged an energy drink and crushed the can. "Let's get the team ready."

Chapter 22

The Sense of Self glowed in the distance, its light growing closer even though the core Emotions still had a long way to go. They had finally reached the end of the Long Term stacks, and they came upon a colorful entrance to what looked like a theme park.

"Imagination Land!" Joy exclaimed. She and Sadness had been there once before, when they'd been lost during their first adventure together, but unlike at the Vault or the Stream of Consciousness, there was nothing scary here. Imagination Land was a wonderful place filled with whimsy and color and fun. "Oh, you guys are going to love it." Joy led the way. "There's French Fry Forest and Cloud Town and—"

She stopped short, taking in her surroundings. Imagination Land might have still been there, but it was *not* the same.

"Whoa, this place has changed," Joy said. Gone were the balloon animals riding sparkling waterslides and the gummy bear parades. Instead, there were fashion boutiques and movie star posters and even a mountain with the faces of four boys, one of which looked like Lance Slashblade, carved into it.

"That must be . . . 'Mount Crushmore'?" Joy said, reading a plaque at the base of the monument.

"*Those* are her top four?" Fear asked doubtfully.

"The only one that matters is Lance," Disgust said dreamily.

"Well, at least they got his good side," muttered Joy.

"*Every* side is his good side," Disgust said with a sigh.

A series of tabloid leaflets drifted down around them, scattered by the turbines of an old-timey windmill nearby. It was the Rumor Mill, which Joy remembered from Forgetter Paula's article about Bree and Grace.

Some Mind Newsies were distributing more pages nearby. "Extra! Extra! Read all about it! Piping hot rumors right off the Mill!"

Disgust grabbed one of the pages. "Abbie R.'s been texting Mike T., but Mike T.'s been flexing for Sarah M."

"I knew it!" said Fear with a gasp.

"Where's the journalistic integrity?" Anger grumbled.

Joy picked up another paper. "'Val laughs at Riley's jokes. But did she mean it?' Ugh! Why is Riley worrying about that?" She crumpled up the paper and tossed it aside.

Then she noticed a large building in the distance. "Oh! Fort Pillowton's still here! This is a really good place to jump around. And it even got bigger!"

"And . . . orange," Disgust said. She then noticed some Mind Workers pushing a cart of office supplies inside the fort.

"What is it?" asked Joy.

"Everything else here has changed," said Disgust. "Why is that still here?"

Curiosity and concern getting the better of them, the Emotions pushed through the poofy orange pillow wall. Joy gasped. Inside was a massive room of cubicles, each one occupied by Mind Workers furiously drawing pictures and scanning them into machines that projected the images onto screens around the room. And in the center was the biggest screen of all, showing none other than Anxiety.

"We need to help Riley prepare!" she commanded the workers. "Now's the time to send up every possible thing that could go wrong."

The workers scribbled furiously, sending their projections up to the screens.

"We're looking to the future," Anxiety continued. "Every possible mistake she could make." She noticed a blank screen. "Come on, Seventeen! I'm not seeing anything from you!"

A stressed Mind Worker scrambled to complete the projection.

"Riley misses an open goal. Coach writes about it in her notebook," said Anxiety. "Yes, great! I love the aggressive underlining. I need more like that!"

The core Emotions watched in dismay as projection after projection popped up on the screens. Anxiety sent the best ones to Riley, overwhelming her with a cascade of terrible images. Riley falling on the ice. Bree and Grace's team winning, making Riley look like a loser. Val laughing at her, saying she was such a little girl for thinking she could make the team.

"They're using Riley's imagination against her!" Disgust said with a gasp.

From her giant screen, Anxiety shouted down to the workers. "Val and her friends like us now! But if we don't make the team, will they like us tomorrow?"

"We can't let her do this to Riley!" Joy said, knowing

that their girl was tossing and turning in her bed. "We have to shut this down."

"But what can we do?" Disgust asked. "There are four of us and like three hundred of them!"

Instinctively, Joy rushed to an empty cubicle and started drawing.

"Why are you drawing a hippo?" Anger asked.

"That's Riley!" Joy said, a bit offended.

"Joy, you forgot her ponytail," Disgust pointed out.

"Oh, good idea!" Joy scribbled the rest of her drawing and scanned it into the projector, sending the image up to Screen 81.

Anxiety saw the image pop up, and she frowned. "Riley scores and everyone hugs her? Eighty-one, that's not helping!"

The other Emotions got in on the projection action, too.

"Riley paints her nails to match her jersey. Everyone copies her! She is so cool!" Disgust sent her image up to the screen.

"Riley wears kneepads!" Fear's drawing was a little jittery but not half bad.

"We buy flowers for the losing team!" Anger drew furiously. He looked up when he realized the others were staring at him. "What? I can't always be the rage guy."

Meanwhile, Anxiety was not pleased with the incoming positive projections. "Nail polish? Kneepads? Do you all understand the assignment?"

At that moment, Embarrassment threw an empty energy drink can across the room. Anxiety looked toward the noise, allowing Embarrassment to hit a button on the console. Anger's projection of Riley buying flowers went to Riley. She stopped tossing and turning and instead had a slight smile on her face.

Embarrassment quickly took his hand off the console as Anxiety whirled around. "Who sent that projection to Riley?"

"Why would I know that?" said Ennui.

"How should I know?" added Envy.

Embarrassment looked back at Sadness in her hiding spot. She gave him a smile and a thumbs-up.

"What is going on?" said Anxiety. "Who's sending up all this positive—" She stopped, her eyes narrowing. "Joy." She moved closer on the screen, giving the sense that she was looming over all the Mind Workers and was ready to pounce. "I know you're in there."

"Whoa, is she really here? Joy from Headquarters?" The Mind Workers began to murmur.

"Well, you're cut off!" Anxiety cut the feed from Joy's projector. "The Mind Police are on their way."

That only made Joy more determined. She stood up on her desk and addressed the Mind Workers. "Don't listen to Anxiety! She's using these horrible projections to change Riley!"

"Joy, I'm doing this for *you*!" Anxiety retorted. "This is so Riley can be happier."

"If you wanted her to be happy, then you'd stop hurting her!" Joy held her arms out wide to the Mind Workers. "Who's with me?"

The workers looked at her skeptically, remaining silent. Someone coughed.

"Really? Nothing?" Joy slumped a little.

"Sorry, Joy," Anxiety said.

But then a fresh image popped up on a projection screen. Number 87 had drawn Riley with a cat.

"Yeah! I see you, Eighty-seven!" Joy cheered. "A cat! A little off topic, but I'll take it! Who else? Come on!"

"What if Riley is better than Val, and so Val hates her?" Anxiety jumped in to grab everyone's attention.

"*Or* . . . what if Riley is better than Val, and Val *respects* her!" Joy countered.

Anxiety and Joy shouted ideas back and forth, each vying for the workers' loyalty.

"What if Riley is so bad she has to give up hockey forever?"

"What if Riley does so well that the coach cries! And the Olympics call, and she rallies a weary nation to victory!"

More and more positive projections began popping up on the screens, infuriating Anxiety.

"Ugh—noooo!" she cried.

Anger leapt up to join Joy on the desk. "Anxiety has got you all chained to desks, drawing nightmares! But you don't have to take it anymore!"

"Pencils down, projections off!" Joy shouted.

"Yeah!" the workers cheered. Some of them began pushing their projectors off their desks, smashing them on the ground.

"Enough is enough!" some started shouting. They grabbed pillows and hurled them across the room. Feathers flew everywhere. It was a full-on pillow fort riot!

"Ahh! My projections!" Anxiety wailed as the screens all went blank. "Curse that sunny-side up vigilante—"

Anxiety's voice cut off as her own screen blacked out and everything dimmed in Fort Pillowton. Riley had finally fallen asleep.

Joy was relieved, but the chaos was still in full swing. Projectors went flying, along with plumes of pillow fluff.

"Okay, it's time to go," Fear said.

"Yeah, I think so," Joy agreed.

Just then, the Mind Police stormed the fort. Mind Workers linked arms, refusing to let them cross the picket line, but the cops had spotted Joy and were heading straight for the Emotions.

Anger grinned and raised his fists. "Bring it on, coppers!"

"Oh, no, no, no," Joy said, lowering his fists. "We need to get out of here!"

The Emotions sprinted after Joy.

"We got Riley to sleep!" Disgust cheered.

"What now?" asked Fear, looking over his shoulder at the dozens of Mind cops headed their way.

"Quick! To the Parade of Future Careers!" Joy shouted.

She led them to a section just outside Fort Pillowton where a long line of oversized parade balloons floated, tethered to the ground. Each one was shaped like Riley in a different future career.

"Grab a balloon!" Joy instructed them.

"The pastry chef one!" Disgust pointed to a balloon shaped like baker Riley.

"Underpaid!" Joy said.

"Art teacher!" Fear pointed to a balloon depicting Riley with an art palette.

"Underappreciated!" Joy said.

"Ethnomusicologist!" Anger grabbed hold of a balloon showing Riley holding a pair of hand drums and a sheet of music.

"Don't know what that is!" Joy said. Then she spotted the biggest balloon of all, which was clearly the winner. "Ooh! Supreme Court justice! Grab on!"

Together, the Emotions untethered the balloon and ran through the streets of Imagination Land, their feet lifting off the ground as the balloon began to soar.

"Stop right there!" The Mind cops blew their whistles. But they were too late. Joy and the Emotions were sailing higher and higher to safety.

"Here we go!" Joy cried, pointing the way to the Sense of Self beacon. "Just don't look down!"

Fear looked down. "*Ahhh!* I miss the jar!"

Chapter 23

In the darkened Headquarters, Anxiety fumed. She had worked *so* hard on those projections. But of course Joy had ruined everything with her glass-half-full, everything-will-work-out-for-the-best attitude. "Joy doesn't get it. Without our projections, we won't be prepared. Tomorrow's game is everything!"

Envy nodded. "Coach will either make us a Fire Hawk or doom us to a friendless future."

"I wish we knew what Coach thought of us," Anxiety said quietly. "Then we could know how to impress her."

Envy's eyes grew wide. "Her notebook!"

"Yes!" Anxiety smiled. "Yes! That's a great idea!" She quickly recalled the memory of the Fire Hawks telling Riley the importance of the notebook.

Everything Coach thinks about you is in there. Whether she wants you on the team . . . or not.

The memory did exactly what Anxiety hoped it would: it jolted Riley awake. With a flicker, the lights brightened inside HQ.

Anxiety's hands flew over the console controls. "All we've got to do is sneak into Coach's office and read it."

But Riley didn't move. She stayed in bed, only shifting to glance at the time: 3:00 a.m.

"Come on, Riley, move those feet!" Anxiety urged her while frantically hitting buttons on the console.

"She doesn't want to?" Envy said, confused.

Anxiety frowned. Her curiosity about Coach's notebook was almost unbearable, but forcing Riley down that path didn't seem like the best solution.

"Are we pushing her too hard?" Anxiety said, hesitating.

"We gotta see what's in the notebook!" Envy insisted. "It's the only way for us to know how we can do better!"

That was all the motivation Riley needed. She got out of bed, pulled on a hoodie, and left her dorm room.

Unseen by either Envy or Anxiety, Sadness witnessed the whole exchange. She gasped.

"Oh, Riley, no," she moaned. "This is really, really bad. I have to do something!"

CHAPTER 23

Over the deserted wasteland leading to the very back of Riley's mind, Joy, Fear, Disgust, and Anger clung to the ropes of their Supreme Court justice Riley balloon. Daylight had returned to the Mind World, indicating that Riley was awake again.

What is happening to our girl? Joy worried to herself.

Suddenly, her walkie-talkie crackled to life. "Joy, come in, Joy."

Joy pulled the walkie-talkie out of her pocket. "Sadness? Sadness? What's wrong? Why is Riley awake again? Over."

For a moment, there was only static on the other end.

"You're breaking up!" Joy shouted.

"Anxiety is making Riley break into the coach's office!" Sadness cried.

"What?" Joy exclaimed.

"She knows better than that!" Anger interjected.

"She will once we get her Sense of Self back!" Disgust said, pointing toward the Back of the Mind.

Joy's imagination went into overdrive, and she thought of all the terrible things Anxiety could do to Riley.

They needed to find her Sense of Self as soon as possible. Joy held the walkie-talkie to her mouth. "Sadness, you have to stop her! Just don't get caught. Over!"

The empty halls of the hockey arena seemed eerie in the dead of night. Riley shivered as she entered through a fortuitously unlocked door. The latch echoed a little too loudly as it closed. *This is really dangerous,* she thought. What if someone spotted her? What if Coach caught her? She could get kicked out of the skills camp—or worse.

But she hadn't been able to get rid of the idea that if she just *knew* what Coach was thinking about her, everything would be all right. If Coach had written that she was doing a good job, she would just keep doing what she was doing. If Coach had written that she needed to focus on her footwork, Riley would do that in the next day's game. (Actually, *that* day's game, seeing as it was almost four o'clock in the morning.)

She tiptoed up to Coach Roberts's office door and tried the handle. *Yes!* It was unlocked.

But then she heard footsteps echoing somewhere

down the hall. Her heartbeat quickened. Someone else was there!

A flashlight skimmed the wall, and she realized with a sickening feeling that a security guard was about to come around the corner.

Gah! She couldn't get caught! Holy cow—would the guard call the police?

As quick as she could, Riley slipped inside Coach's office and locked the door behind her. Then she crouched down low, making herself as small as possible so she wouldn't be spotted through the door's window.

Scarcely breathing, she listened as the guard's footsteps approached the door. She could see his flashlight shine through the window above her, and she shrank down farther in the shadows. The guard tried the door handle and found it locked. For an agonizingly long moment, he remained by the door, shining his flashlight inside.

Then, finally, he moved off down the hall.

Riley exhaled, her entire body shaking violently.

This was a mistake. This was a mistake this was a mistake this was a mistake.

But she was there now, and the notebook was on Coach's desk just an arm's length away.

Riley crept over and picked up the book. She held it in her hands and stared at Coach's firm handwriting on the cover, each letter so official.

Everything she needed to know was in there. And yet . . .

Riley's chest felt heavy, and tears formed in the corners of her eyes.

What was she doing? Who *was* she anymore? She felt like she didn't even know herself. Riley looked at a mirror and saw her reflection. Her blond hair was ashy in the office security lights, and her skin was sallow. Was this who she really was?

"What happened?" Anxiety asked. She went to push some buttons on the console and saw that the entire thing was glowing watery blue.

"Sadness?" Anxiety said, confused. She looked up and around the console, but there was no one there except her, Envy, Embarrassment, and Ennui, whose eyes were uncharacteristically riveted to the screen.

"Ennui, where's your phone?" Anxiety asked slowly.

With a gasp, Ennui checked her pockets.

"Ooh la la, my phone," she said, panicking. "Where is my phone? Seriously! This is not happening!"

Anxiety put two and two together. Somehow, Sadness was in HQ, and she was driving the console with Ennui's phone app.

"She's here somewhere," Anxiety said. "Find her!"

Anxiety, Envy, and Ennui began scouring Headquarters while Embarrassment attempted to hang back, not wanting to reveal Sadness's hiding spot.

Envy and Ennui approached the hidden corner with the stacks of manuals. Embarrassment gasped and pulled his hoodie over his eyes.

"Gotcha!" Envy exclaimed.

Sadness wasn't there. Embarrassment exhaled in relief.

But within moments, Anxiety spotted a soft light coming from the Emotions' bedroom. The glow of Ennui's phone emanating through the bedcovers had given away the little blue Emotion.

"Sadness?" Anxiety said softly.

"Um, no?" Sadness squeaked.

Anxiety yanked the covers off Sadness and took the phone away.

"I know Riley sneaking around feels wrong," Anxiety said, sitting next to Sadness.

"This isn't who Riley is," Sadness pleaded.

"It's not about who Riley is. It's about who she needs to be."

"No, I won't let you do this," Sadness said, trying to keep the tremble out of her voice.

Anxiety sighed. "Desperate times call for desperate measures."

A couple of minutes later, a restrained Sadness sat in a bucket. Using a pulley and rope, Anxiety raised the bucket to the ceiling of Headquarters, trapping Sadness midair.

"Sorry, Sadness," Anxiety said as she tied off the rope. "I don't want to do this, either."

Then Anxiety returned to the console.

In Coach's office, Riley finally stopped crying. She looked down again at the notebook. *This may not feel right, but it is the only way,* she told herself. Just this one time, she would do something a little wrong so that she could make sure things went a lot right.

Before she could second-guess herself again, Riley flipped through the pages, scanning Coach Roberts's scribbled notes until—

She let out a strangled cry.

The words were right there, plain as day. She couldn't unsee them now.

ANDERSEN: NOT READY YET

Riley's hand flew to her mouth.

She had wanted to know, and now she did.

But she had never imagined that her chances of being a Fire Hawk were already gone.

Chapter 24

"This. Can't. Be. Happening," Envy said, distraught. "We have one day left!"

Anxiety was so shocked she couldn't even vibrate like normal. "Wait, Coach already decided? We're not making the team?"

"What do we do?" Envy started to panic. "What *can* we do? What would Val do?"

"Okay, okay, okay," Anxiety said, gripping her hair. "We're gonna have to change Coach's mind. Which means we're gonna need ideas. *Lots* of them."

Anxiety cranked levers and spun wheels on the console, sending a tremor through the whole of Headquarters. In the distance, a there was a rumbling sound, and the recall tubes leading into HQ rattled ominously.

"Look! We're so close, you guys!" Joy shouted to the Emotions.

"Woo! Yeah!" Fear cheered.

Seeing the glow from the Sense of Self in the distance reminded them that the old Riley—*their* Riley—was still alive. And that meant hope was alive, too.

Somewhere behind them, there was a sound like thunder, and dark storm clouds started rolling in.

"Uhhhh . . ." Fear said nervously.

Idea bulbs began pouring from the sky, hitting the Emotions on their heads and bouncing precariously off the balloon.

"Oh, no, it's a brainstorm!" warned Anger.

Lightning crackled across the sky as more and more ideas rained down. Joy grabbed a few as they flew past.

"Hog the puck? Trash-talk the other team?" she said, analyzing each one. "We can't let these bad ideas get to Riley!"

Ideas were pouring into Headquarters, and Embarrassment raced between the tubes, collecting them in large buckets.

Envy was thrilled. "I'll start sorting these into 'Ideas I Wish I'd Thought Of.' "

Anxiety sifted through the piles, growing more annoyed as she did so. "No, no, no! None of these are good enough! We need more! Get more!"

Joy grabbed the wooden stake that was tied to the bottom of her rope. She started using it to shatter all the bad ideas that flew past her.

"Smash as many as you can!" she called to the other Emotions.

But Disgust, Anger, and Fear watched as the balloon moved closer and closer to the center of the fierce brainstorm.

"We need to steer around it!" Disgust cried. She pointed out a path that would lead them away from the storm and back toward the Sense of Self.

"Everybody, get on this side!" Anger shouted.

Disgust and Fear moved over to Anger's rope. Their combined weight tilted the balloon slightly to the right. But it wasn't enough. They needed more weight.

"Joy!" Anger called.

But Joy was single-minded in her goal. She ignored Anger and continued to swing at the idea bulbs.

"Joy!" Anger shouted more urgently.

It was too late. The wind pulled them into the storm and spun the balloon around and around. The Emotions clung to the ropes.

"Get on the balloon!" Disgust exclaimed.

The group climbed to the top of the balloon as lightning flashed and ideas rained down.

"This is worse than the broccoli," Disgust groaned, somehow looking even greener than usual.

Anger shut his eyes. "I hate this so much."

"We're gonna die!" Fear shrieked.

"Oh, stop saying that!" Disgust cried.

Fear tried to calm himself down. He looked up and noticed the ideas leaving the storm through tubes bound for Headquarters.

"The only way out is up!" he shouted. "Quick, grab an idea!"

Disgust caught a medium-sized idea and held it aloft. It lifted her for a moment but quickly sank back down to the balloon.

Anger shook his head. "These ideas are too small. We need something bigger!"

As though he had spoken it into existence, a massive idea zoomed toward the Emotions.

"That's our way out!" Fear said.

The three Emotions watched and waited for the big idea to fly closer. Suddenly, it slammed right into them! Before the bulb could zoom away with the Emotions in tow, Joy brought it to a halt and prepared to smash it.

"Wait!" Fear exclaimed. "We need this idea!"

"If Riley takes one of these ideas, it could be a disaster!" Joy insisted, still holding the wooden stake above her head.

"Joy, worst case, she'll live," said Fear. "I can't say the same for us!"

Although she was still hesitant, Joy couldn't argue with Fear's logic. She nodded and dropped the stake.

The Emotions held on to the big idea. It rose in the air, zoomed out of the storm, and headed toward a tube. The Emotions had no choice but to jump off.

"Ahhh!" they all screamed.

The giant idea bulb squeezed into Headquarters, distending the recall tube with its girth. It was so big it crushed

Embarrassment's collection bucket, spilling smaller, shattered idea bulbs everywhere.

Anxiety and Envy rushed over to the colossal idea. It reflected their eyes as they watched the images playing inside, which suggested a course of action for Riley.

"*That's* a big idea!" Anxiety cheered.

"Oooh, I like it," Envy agreed.

No one had ever before done anything as big as this idea at skills camp.

This idea would change everything.

Most important, it was guaranteed to change Coach's mind.

Anxiety was certain.

The Emotions plummeted to the ground.

"Hold me!" Fear shrieked. Then, more insistently, he repeated, *"Hold me!"*

Everyone grabbed on to Fear when suddenly . . .

POOF!

A parachute deployed, gliding them gently through the air.

"Fear!" Joy exclaimed in surprise.

Disgust was equally stunned. She looked up at him. "You have a parachute?"

"Uh, yeah," Fear said as though it was a silly question. "The real question is, why don't any of you?"

The Emotions landed softly on the ground and brushed themselves off.

"Stuck the landing!" Fear exclaimed.

"We did it!" Anger cheered.

Disgust sighed in relief. "We made it!"

Joy tried not to think about what Anxiety could do with all those terrible ideas. But she couldn't dwell on it for too long. She turned to the Sense of Self in the distance. "Come on! To the Back of the Mind! You're finished, Anxiety!"

She and the Emotions gathered their remaining strength and dashed toward the Back of the Mind.

ADNESS•ANGER•ANXIETY•DISGUST•EMBARRASSMENT•ENNUI•ENVY•FEAR
MBARRASSMENT•ENNUI•ENVY•FEAR•JOY•SADNESS•ANGER•ANXIETY•DISG
NESS•ANGER•ANXIETY•DISGUST•EMBARRASSMENT•ENNUI•ENVY•FEAR•JOY
MBARRASSMENT•ENNUI•ENVY•FEAR•JOY•SADNESS•ANGER•ANXIETY•DISGU
FEAR•JOY•SADNESS•ANGER•ANXIETY•DISGUST•EMBARRASSMENT•ENNUI•E
ENVY•FEAR•JOY•SADNESS•ANGER•ANXIETY•DISGUST•EMBARRASSMENT•EM
NXIETY•DISGUST•EMBARRASSMENT•ENNUI•ENVY•FEAR•JOY•SADNESS•ANG
MENT•ENNUI•ENVY•FEAR•JOY•SADNESS•ANXIETY•DISGUST•EMBARRASSM
ETY•DISGUST•EMBARRASSMENT•ENNUI•ENVY•FEAR•JOY•SADNESS•ANGER
ENT•ENNUI•ENVY•FEAR•JOY•SADNESS•ANGER•ANXIETY•DISGUST•EMBAR
•ANGER•ANXIETY•DISGUST•EMBARRASSMENT•ENNUI•ENVY•FEAR•JOY•SA
RASSMENT•ENNUI•ENVY•FEAR•JOY•SADNESS•ANXIETY•DISGUST•EMBARRA
SADNESS•ANGER•ANXIETY•DISGUST•EMBARRASSMENT•ENNUI•ENVY•FEAR
MBARRASSMENT•ENNUI•ENVY•FEAR•JOY•SADNESS•ANGER•ANXIETY•DISG
NESS•ANGER•ANXIETY•DISGUST•EMBARRASSMENT•ENNUI•ENVY•FEAR•JO
MBARRASSMENT•ENNUI•ENVY•FEAR•JOY•SADNESS•ANGER•ANXIETY•DISGU
FEAR•JOY•SADNESS•ANGER•ANXIETY•DISGUST•EMBARRASSMENT•ENNUI•E
ENVY•FEAR•JOY•SADNESS•ANGER•ANXIETY•DISGUST•EMBARRASSMENT•EN
NXIETY•DISGUST•EMBARRASSMENT•ENNUI•ENVY•FEAR•JOY•SADNESS•ANG
MENT•ENNUI•ENVY•FEAR•JOY•SADNESS•ANXIETY•DISGUST•EMBARRASSM
ETY•DISGUST•EMBARRASSMENT•ENNUI•ENVY•FEAR•JOY•SADNESS•ANGER
ENT•ENNUI•ENVY•FEAR•JOY•SADNESS•ANGER•ANXIETY•DISGUST•EMBARR
•ANGER•ANXIETY•DISGUST•EMBARRASSMENT•ENNUI•ENVY•FEAR•JOY•SA
RASSMENT•ENNUI•ENVY•FEAR•JOY•SADNESS•ANXIETY•DISGUST•EMBARR
SADNESS•ANGER•ANXIETY•DISGUST•EMBARRASSMENT•ENNUI•ENVY•FEAR
MBARRASSMENT•ENNUI•ENVY•FEAR•JOY•SADNESS•ANGER•ANXIETY•DIS
NESS•ANGER•ANXIETY•DISGUST•EMBARRASSMENT•ENNUI•ENVY•FEAR•JO
MBARRASSMENT•ENNUI•ENVY•FEAR•JOY•SADNESS•ANGER•ANXIETY•DISG
FEAR•JOY•SADNESS•ANGER•ANXIETY•DISGUST•EMBARRASSMENT•ENNUI•E
ENVY•FEAR•JOY•SADNESS•ANGER•ANXIETY•DISGUST•EMBARRASSMENT•AN
NXIETY•DISGUST•EMBARRASSMENT•ENNUI•ENVY•FEAR•JOY•SADNESS•ANG
MENT•ENNUI•ENVY•FEAR•JOY•SADNESS•ANXIETY•DISGUST•EMBARRASSM
ETY•DISGUST•EMBARRASSMENT•ENNUI•ENVY•FEAR•JOY•SADNESS•ANGER
ENT•ENNUI•ENVY•FEAR•JOY•SADNESS•ANGER•ANXIETY•DISGUST•EMBARR
•ANGER•ANXIETY•DISGUST•EMBARRASSMENT•ENNUI•ENVY•FEAR•JOY•SA
RASSMENT•ENNUI•ENVY•FEAR•JOY•SADNESS•ANXIETY•DISGUST•EMBARRA

Chapter 25

The moment had finally arrived: it was game time. Anxiety picked up the big idea and lugged it to the console.

"Coach is right. Riley isn't ready," Anxiety said. "But we're so close to a new Riley who is. This is what we're missing. We show them we're a Fire Hawk who will do whatever it takes." She plugged the idea into the console.

In the locker room, Riley began her preparations—starting with her hair. All it had taken was some conditioner and an entire packet of Cherry Quencher powder to add the signature streak of fiery red to Riley's sandy-blond locks. Riley flipped her hair, showing off her handiwork.

"Finally! We're one of them!" Envy cheered. She and Anxiety shared a high five. Anxiety looked up at Sadness in the bucket. "What do you think, Sadness?"

"Well, I—"

"Awesome!" Anxiety exclaimed, leaping with excitement.

"Red is really our color," Envy said as she nodded in approval.

At that moment, Grace and Bree made their way into the locker room.

"Trust me!" Grace said with a smile.

Bree laughed. "Yeah, I know. I mean, it's so much fun."

They stopped short when they caught sight of Riley. They turned away from her and busied themselves at their lockers.

"Okay, it's giving jealousy," said Envy.

Ennui rolled her eyes. "They wouldn't know cool if it hit them in the face."

Val and some of the Fire Hawks arrived next. Val raised an eyebrow at Riley's new look. "Hey, Michigan. Rockin' the red, huh?"

"I hope it's okay," Riley said. "I know I'm not officially a Fire Hawk yet, but I figured since we're on the same team today, we should match, right?"

"Yeah, yeah, that's fine." Val noticed the dark circles under Riley's eyes. "Did you sleep last night?"

"No!" Riley said brightly. "How could I? Big game today!"

"You mean the camp scrimmage?" another Fire Hawk said, glancing up at her.

"Leave her alone. She's in her zone," Val said. She gave Riley a thumbs-up. "Get ready to score some goals!"

"See?" Anxiety exclaimed. "Val is the only one who understands!"

Envy climbed up to the console. "So what's the plan for the game?"

"Val scored two goals in this scrimmage to become a Fire Hawk," Anxiety stated.

Envy nodded. "So we need to score two goals to be just like her!"

"Actually, Envy," said Anxiety, "you know what's better than two? Three!"

"Three!" Envy exclaimed. "I was just about to say that. We were about to say that at the same time."

In her spot on the couch, Ennui deigned to glance up. "And how are we going to score three goals?"

Anxiety stretched her arms and twisted from side to side. She needed to be warmed up, too. "The new Riley will handle anything. And I think *this* is the finishing touch." She picked up the orange memory sphere of Riley showing off her new hair. Then she headed to the Belief System elevator. "I'll be right back."

Joy and the Emotions climbed a steep hill in the Back of the Mind.

"Are we there yet?" Fear gasped in exhaustion.

"How much farther?" Anger panted.

"Almost there, guys!" Joy said, urging them on. "I can feel it. Look!" She could see the hill's peak. She turned to the others. "C'mon, grab my hand. You got it!"

Joy helped the other Emotions reach the top, which would give them a full view of the Back of the Mind.

"We're so close!" Joy said encouragingly. "The Sense of Self is just on top of that—" She turned around to see the landscape. "Mountain," Joy finished quietly.

But this was no mountain. It was a massive pile of discarded memory spheres. There were hundreds—perhaps thousands—of them, each one replaying a memory Joy had deemed harmful to Riley.

"That is a lot," Fear said in shock.

"This is more than I remember sending back here," Joy murmured.

She processed the enormity of the pile. Sure, she'd been doing a little mind-scaping every night. A cringeworthy memory here, an "oof, that's hurtful" recollection there. She honestly hadn't realized how many she'd placed into the tube, but they must have added up over time.

Disgust noticed a memory nearby. "Oh, when she walked into that glass door at that party? Oof."

Joy picked up another one. "Yeah, and breaking Grandma's favorite plate? Thank goodness these aren't part of her."

Fear, Anger, and Disgust nodded in agreement and followed Joy as they began to climb the mountain.

Orange luminescence from the new belief strings radiated throughout the Belief System. Anxiety tossed the memory sphere into the water and returned to the elevator. An enormous pulse of energy surged from the swirling water.

The core Emotions struggled up the mountain. Joy dug through the endless pile of memories as they went. She knew the Sense of Self had to be there somewhere.

Finally, she unearthed a glowing flower-like object.

"There it is!" Joy cried, picking it up.

I'm a good person.

All at once, Joy felt an overwhelming rush of feelings. It was Riley—their Riley. They had found her old Sense of Self. But its light dimmed, and Riley's voice grew faint.

"Oh, no!" Joy exclaimed.

There was one more thing left to do.

"We gotta get to the tube," said Joy.

Anxiety arrived back in HQ just as the entire room filled with orange light. She watched in triumph as the final belief strings intertwined with the others, revealing a new, brilliant, perfect, better-than-ever-before Sense of Self.

"Yes. Come on. Come on," Anxiety muttered under her breath.

The Sense of Self glowed with orange light and hummed with energy.

"Here we go!" Anxiety exclaimed.

I'M NOT GOOD ENOUGH.

"W-what?" Anxiety said in surprise and confusion.

"Why does it say that?" Envy asked. The other Emotions looked equally confused and concerned.

"Uh, um—" Anxiety stammered, "don't worry! It's just that she knows there's always room for self-improvement! She'll be fine!"

The other Emotions shared uncertain glances as Anxiety walked back to the console and cracked her knuckles.

Suddenly, Sadness heard Joy's voice from the walkie-talkie. "Sadness, we have the Sense of Self. Bring us back!"

Anxiety was too preoccupied at the console to hear Joy's command, but Embarrassment heard every word. Sadness looked down at him, silently begging for help. Embarrassment glanced from her to Anxiety.

I'M NOT GOOD ENOUGH, the Sense of Self announced again.

A look of determination crossed Embarrassment's face. Finally, he lowered Sadness's bucket to the ground and freed her from the restraints. Sadness smiled at him in gratitude. She then signaled him to the Back of the Mind tube. Embarrassment nodded in understanding.

Sadness snuck toward the console while Embarrassment moved to the tube. They watched Anxiety closely, waiting for the right moment.

"Okay, I can work with this," Anxiety muttered to herself. "I just need to recalibrate the console and make sure it's ready. Just no more surprises." She began fiddling with the console. "Uh, okay, this one goes here. Check. That one goes there. Check. No, not exactly there."

With Anxiety's focus on the console, Embarrassment took his chance and lowered the tube. Sadness slowly reached over to the recall button.

"Sadness, now!" Joy exclaimed over the walkie-talkie.

Anxiety looked up and saw Sadness's hand on the button. *"Ahh!"* she screamed.

Then, to her horror, she realized Embarrassment was standing next to the Back of the Mind tube. She rushed to the tube and used the long hook to rip the entire contraption right out of the ceiling. It clattered to the floor, destroyed. Sadness could hear the remainder of the tube crumbling with a ripple effect way out beyond Headquarters.

It was over. There was no way to bring back her friends now.

At the peak of the mountain of memory spheres, Joy waited for a sign from Sadness. *What if Sadness got caught?* she wondered. *What if she didn't hear my message?*

Joy heard a whoosh of air overhead from the Back of the Mind tube. It was turned on!

"She did it!" Joy cheered. "Good ol' Sadness!"

But before Joy could lift the Sense of Self to the tube opening, Fear pointed at Headquarters with a trembling hand. "Oh, no . . ." he whimpered.

Joy and the others watched as the Back of the Mind tube dropped from the sky in the distance. Finally, the last remnants of the tube crashed in front of them. They dodged the debris as memory spheres scattered and flew around them. The Mind World settled into silence.

"It . . . it can't be," Anger said in disbelief. "That was our only way back."

Disgust looked out at Headquarters, with its orange light radiating across the landscape. "But . . . we came so far. We were so close."

"Oh, Riley," Joy whispered, devastated.

DNESS·ANGER·ANXIETY·DISGUST·EMBARRASSMENT·ENNUI·ENV
MBARRASSMENT·ENNUI·ENVY·FEAR·JOY·SADNESS·ANGER·ANXIETY·DISGU
ESS·ANGER·ANXIETY·DISGUST·EMBARRASSMENT·ENNUI·ENVY·FEAR·JOY
MBARRASSMENT·ENNUI·ENVY·FEAR·JOY·SADNESS·ANGER·ANXIETY·DISGU
EAR·JOY·SADNESS·ANGER·ANXIETY·DISGUST·EMBARRASSMENT·ENNUI·EN
NVY·FEAR·JOY·SADNESS·ANGER·ANXIETY·DISGUST·EMBARRASSMENT·EN
XIETY·DISGUST·EMBARRASSMENT·ENNUI·ENVY·FEAR·JOY·SADNESS·ANG
ENT·ENNUI·ENVY·FEAR·JOY·SADNESS·ANXIETY·DISGUST·EMBARRASSME
TY·DISGUST·EMBARRASSMENT·ENNUI·ENVY·FEAR·JOY·SADNESS·ANGER·
ENT·ENNUI·ENVY·FEAR·JOY·SADNESS·ANGER·ANXIETY·DISGUST·EMBARRA
ANGER·ANXIETY·DISGUST·EMBARRASSMENT·ENNUI·ENVY·FEAR·JOY·SAD
ASSMENT·ENNUI·ENVY·FEAR·JOY·SADNESS·ANXIETY·DISGUST·EMBARRAS
ADNESS·ANGER·ANXIETY·DISGUST·EMBARRASSMENT·ENNUI·ENVY·FEAR·
MBARRASSMENT·ENNUI·ENVY·FEAR·JOY·SADNESS·ANGER·ANXIETY·DISGU
ESS·ANGER·ANXIETY·DISGUST·EMBARRASSMENT·ENNUI·ENVY·FEAR·JOY
MBARRASSMENT·ENNUI·ENVY·FEAR·JOY·SADNESS·ANGER·ANXIETY·DISGU
EAR·JOY·SADNESS·ANGER·ANXIETY·DISGUST·EMBARRASSMENT·ENNUI·EN
NVY·FEAR·JOY·SADNESS·ANGER·ANXIETY·DISGUST·EMBARRASSMENT·EN
XIETY·DISGUST·EMBARRASSMENT·ENNUI·ENVY·FEAR·JOY·SADNESS·ANG
ENT·ENNUI·ENVY·FEAR·JOY·SADNESS·ANXIETY·DISGUST·EMBARRASSME
TY·DISGUST·EMBARRASSMENT·ENNUI·ENVY·FEAR·JOY·SADNESS·ANGER·
ENT·ENNUI·ENVY·FEAR·JOY·SADNESS·ANGER·ANXIETY·DISGUST·EMBARRA
ANGER·ANXIETY·DISGUST·EMBARRASSMENT·ENNUI·ENVY·FEAR·JOY·SAD
ASSMENT·ENNUI·ENVY·FEAR·JOY·SADNESS·ANXIETY·DISGUST·EMBARRAS
ADNESS·ANGER·ANXIETY·DISGUST·EMBARRASSMENT·ENNUI·ENVY·FEAR·
MBARRASSMENT·ENNUI·ENVY·FEAR·JOY·SADNESS·ANGER·ANXIETY·DISGU
ESS·ANGER·ANXIETY·DISGUST·EMBARRASSMENT·ENNUI·ENVY·FEAR·JOY
MBARRASSMENT·ENNUI·ENVY·FEAR·JOY·SADNESS·ANGER·ANXIETY·DISGU
EAR·JOY·SADNESS·ANGER·ANXIETY·DISGUST·EMBARRASSMENT·ENNUI·EN
NVY·FEAR·JOY·SADNESS·ANGER·ANXIETY·DISGUST·EMBARRASSMENT·EN
XIETY·DISGUST·EMBARRASSMENT·ENNUI·ENVY·FEAR·JOY·SADNESS·ANG
ENT·ENNUI·ENVY·FEAR·JOY·SADNESS·ANXIETY·DISGUST·EMBARRASSME
TY·DISGUST·EMBARRASSMENT·ENNUI·ENVY·FEAR·JOY·SADNESS·ANGER·
ENT·ENNUI·ENVY·FEAR·JOY·SADNESS·ANGER·ANXIETY·DISGUST·EMBARRA
ANGER·ANXIETY·DISGUST·EMBARRASSMENT·ENNUI·ENVY·FEAR·JOY·SAD
ASSMENT·ENNUI·ENVY·FEAR·JOY·SADNESS·ANXIETY·DISGUST·EMBARRA

Chapter 26

They were too late. They had failed their girl. How would they ever get their Riley back now?

"What do we do? What do we do?" Fear shrieked.

"Her Sense of Self is dying!" Disgust exclaimed.

Riley's new Sense of Self echoed across the Mind World. *I'M NOT GOOD ENOUGH.*

Joy cradled the old Sense of Self in her arms.

I'm a good person, it said faintly.

Without a word, Joy walked away.

"Joy! Joy!" Disgust called. "Where are you going?"

Joy slid a short distance down the mountain. She had no idea where she was going or what she was doing, but she needed a moment alone. Her knees buckled. She dropped to the ground, and her eyes blurred with tears. Colors from the discarded memories were striated in her misty vision, making the memories playing inside look like images in a kaleidoscope. She gazed at the one closest to her: the memory of Riley's penalty from the championship game.

Joy gazed at memory after memory of times Riley had made mistakes and had fallen short—when she had cheated on a test, when she had gotten into an argument with her dad, when she had stolen her mom's credit card . . .

Joy searched through the memories, looking for any clue—any way forward that would allow them to save their girl. She buried her head in her hands. "Come on. Please. What am I missing?"

Joy picked up the fading Sense of Self.

I'm a good person.

Anger, Fear, and Disgust approached Joy.

"Joy, so . . . what do we do now?" Disgust asked cautiously.

"I don't know," Joy replied.

Disgust, Anger, and Fear exchanged worried looks. Joy *always* knew what to do. She always had a bright side, a plan B, or, at the very least, a spontaneous idea that would lead to a real plan. But a hopeless Joy was someone they had never seen before.

"I don't know how to stop Anxiety," Joy continued. "Maybe we can't. Maybe this is what happens when you grow up. You feel less joy."

Joy's heart broke even further with those words. But she knew that even if Riley never needed her again, she would still sacrifice anything for her.

Joy held up the Sense of Self. "I do know this: Riley will never be herself if we don't get this back to Headquarters—fast."

Disgust furrowed her brow. "But . . . how?"

Riley skated to the center of the ice. This was it: her last chance to prove that she had what it took to be a Fire Hawk.

Grace crouched directly across from her. She stared Riley down. "Have a good game, Riley."

"You too," Riley said.

Coach Roberts dropped the puck. Riley's eyes followed the puck down to the ice. She took possession of it and immediately hustled toward the goal.

"Yes! Go, go, go!" Anxiety shouted.

Dani waved at Riley. "Riley! I'm open! Pass it! Pass it!"

Riley's Sense of Self activated. *I'M NOT GOOD ENOUGH.*

She ignored Dani, slipped past a defender, and slapped a shot past Bree. *Goal!*

The Fire Hawks celebrated.

"Yeah, Michigan!" Val cheered. She gave Riley a high five.

"Leave some for the rest of us, huh?" Dani said with a smile.

In Headquarters, an orange memory of the Fire Hawks' celebration rolled out.

"Yes! One down! Two to go!" Anxiety exclaimed.

In the Back of the Mind, the Emotions struggled to come up with a new plan.

Suddenly, Fear perked up. "I got it!"

The other Emotions watched as Fear dropped a memory sphere into the canyon below. It headed toward Headquarters and eventually fell into the Sar-chasm.

"Look!" said Fear. "That Sar-chasm leads to the Stream of Consciousness, which connects to the Belief System!"

Joy thought back to the beautiful rainbow water in

Riley's Belief System that had fed all her belief strings. She had noticed the rainbow splash the broccoli floret made at the bottom of the Sar-chasm. They were one and the same, she had realized. If they could get into that chasm, they would reach the Belief System and be able to take the elevator to Headquarters.

"Okay, so how do we get Riley's Sense of Self from here . . . to there?" Disgust asked. "We don't have time to walk back."

"I . . . didn't get that far," Fear admitted.

Anger sighed. "I have an idea, but I really don't like it."

"Anger," Joy said gently, "Riley needs us."

He took a deep breath. "Oh, Pouchy!"

Nothing happened.

"Well, what are you waiting for?" Anger exclaimed. "Say the words!"

The Emotions shouted at the top of their lungs: *"Oh, Pouchy!"*

A faint glimmer appeared in the sky like a distant star. Then it drew closer and closer to the Emotions, swooping toward them in a stream of sparkles, until the unmistakable cartoon fanny pack was hovering right in front of them.

"Hi, everybody! I'm Pouchy!"

"We know," Anger grumbled.

"Pouchy, we need to get back to Headquarters," Joy explained. "Do you have anything that can help us?"

"I have lots of items!" Pouchy said cheerfully. "Which one do you think will work best? A roll of tape? A rubber ducky? Or—"

"No time!" Anger shouted.

With a lunge, he tackled Pouchy to the ground and shoved his hand right inside the fanny pack's zipper mouth. He reached around, feeling for the right item, amid Pouchy's muffled protests. He pulled out a bundle of dynamite. He reached in again only to pull out more dynamite.

"Seriously, Pouchy? Dynamite?" Disgust exclaimed. "How will that help us? Don't you have like a jet pack or a plane or something in there?"

Pouchy's words were muffled because of Anger's arm. He spit it out. "What? Do you think I have everything in here? I offered you the rubber ducky; I offered you the tape . . ."

Joy looked down at the pile of dynamite. She brightened with an idea. "I know what to do! But we're going to need a lot more dynamite."

Anger cackled as he reached back into Pouchy's mouth.

On the ice rink, it was time to zone in on goal number two.

"Come on, Riley! Get the puck!" Anxiety demanded. "Get the puck! Take it! Take it!"

I'M NOT GOOD ENOUGH.

Riley spotted Dani with the puck. With Anxiety driving hard, Riley attempted to steal the puck away from her.

"Michigan, what are you doing?" Dani said in confusion. "We're on the same team!"

Riley shoved her, took the puck, and sped toward the goal. She smacked the puck past Bree, straight into the net. Coach Roberts wrote something in her notebook.

"That's right, Coach," Envy said smugly. "R-I-L-E-Y! Future Fire Hawk superstar!"

Everything was going according to plan. Riley *would* be a Fire Hawk. Coach couldn't deny her a spot on the team if she scored more goals than any other player ever had in the history of the skills camp.

Val and Dani stared at Riley.

"Okay, well, Dani might be a little mad at us," Anxiety said nervously, "but they'll all forgive us when we make the team. Come on, Riley! One more goal!"

EMBARRASSMENT·ENNUI·ENVY·FEAR·JOY·SADNESS·ANGER·ANXIETY·DISGU
ESS·ANGER·ANXIETY·DISGUST·EMBARRASSMENT·ENNUI·ENVY·FEAR·JOY
BARRASSMENT·ENNUI·ENVY·FEAR·JOY·SADNESS·ANGER·ANXIETY·DISGU
EAR·JOY·SADNESS·ANGER·ANXIETY·DISGUST·EMBARRASSMENT·ENNUI·E
ENVY·FEAR·JOY·SADNESS·ANGER·ANXIETY·DISGUST·EMBARRASSMENT·E
XIETY·DISGUST·EMBARRASSMENT·ENNUI·ENVY·FEAR·JOY·SADNESS·ANG
ENT·ENNUI·ENVY·FEAR·JOY·SADNESS·ANXIETY·DISGUST·EMBARRASSME
TY·DISGUST·EMBARRASSMENT·ENNUI·ENVY·FEAR·JOY·SADNESS·ANGER
NT·ENNUI·ENVY·FEAR·JOY·SADNESS·ANGER·ANXIETY·DISGUST·EMBARR
ANGER·ANXIETY·DISGUST·EMBARRASSMENT·ENNUI·ENVY·FEAR·JOY·SAD
ASSMENT·ENNUI·ENVY·FEAR·JOY·SADNESS·ANXIETY·DISGUST·EMBARRA
ADNESS·ANGER·ANXIETY·DISGUST·EMBARRASSMENT·ENNUI·ENVY·FEAR·
BARRASSMENT·ENNUI·ENVY·FEAR·JOY·SADNESS·ANGER·ANXIETY·DISGU
ESS·ANGER·ANXIETY·DISGUST·EMBARRASSMENT·ENNUI·ENVY·FEAR·JOY
BARRASSMENT·ENNUI·ENVY·FEAR·JOY·SADNESS·ANGER·ANXIETY·DISGU
AR·JOY·SADNESS·ANGER·ANXIETY·DISGUST·EMBARRASSMENT·ENNUI·EN
NVY·FEAR·JOY·SADNESS·ANGER·ANXIETY·DISGUST·EMBARRASSMENT·EN
IETY·DISGUST·EMBARRASSMENT·ENNUI·ENVY·FEAR·JOY·SADNESS·ANG
ENT·ENNUI·ENVY·FEAR·JOY·SADNESS·ANXIETY·DISGUST·EMBARRASSME
TY·DISGUST·EMBARRASSMENT·ENNUI·ENVY·FEAR·JOY·SADNESS·ANGER·
NT·ENNUI·ENVY·FEAR·JOY·SADNESS·ANGER·ANXIETY·DISGUST·EMBARR
ANGER·ANXIETY·DISGUST·EMBARRASSMENT·ENNUI·ENVY·FEAR·JOY·SAD
ASSMENT·ENNUI·ENVY·FEAR·JOY·SADNESS·ANXIETY·DISGUST·EMBARRA
ADNESS·ANGER·ANXIETY·DISGUST·EMBARRASSMENT·ENNUI·ENVY·FEAR
BARRASSMENT·ENNUI·ENVY·FEAR·JOY·SADNESS·ANGER·ANXIETY·DISGU
ESS·ANGER·ANXIETY·DISGUST·EMBARRASSMENT·ENNUI·ENVY·FEAR·JOY
BARRASSMENT·ENNUI·ENVY·FEAR·JOY·SADNESS·ANGER·ANXIETY·DISGU
EAR·JOY·SADNESS·ANGER·ANXIETY·DISGUST·EMBARRASSMENT·ENNUI·EN
ENVY·FEAR·JOY·SADNESS·ANGER·ANXIETY·DISGUST·EMBARRASSMENT·EN
XIETY·DISGUST·EMBARRASSMENT·ENNUI·ENVY·FEAR·JOY·SADNESS·ANG
MENT·ENNUI·ENVY·FEAR·JOY·SADNESS·ANXIETY·DISGUST·EMBARRASSME
TY·DISGUST·EMBARRASSMENT·ENNUI·ENVY·FEAR·JOY·SADNESS·ANGER
NT·ENNUI·ENVY·FEAR·JOY·SADNESS·ANGER·ANXIETY·DISGUST·EMBARR
ANGER·ANXIETY·DISGUST·EMBARRASSMENT·ENNUI·ENVY·FEAR·JOY·SAD
ASSMENT·ENNUI·ENVY·FEAR·JOY·SADNESS·ANXIETY·DISGUST·EMBARRA

Chapter 27

In the Back of the Mind, the Emotions stood in the canyon below the mountain of memory spheres. They had placed all of Pouchy's dynamite around a narrow rock pillar that supported the memory sphere pile.

Joy held the detonator and stared up at the massive mountain. This wasn't her first daring plan. She thought about the time she had used the Imaginary Boyfriend Generator in Imagination Land to form a massive tower of boyfriends that had launched her onto a trampoline and sent her hurtling back to Headquarters. But even that plan seemed sensible compared to this one.

A concerned Disgust approached her. "Uh, wait a minute. Hold on, Joy. We're going to blow up this cliff?"

"Yup!" Joy said simply.

"And then we'll ride an avalanche of bad memories back to Headquarters?"

"Yeah."

"Uh, okay. And how do we keep the bad memories from forming bad beliefs?"

"I don't know."

Disgust shrugged. "Um, yeah. What could go wrong? I'm in!"

The four Emotions got into position.

"Ready?" Joy asked.

Anger smiled at her. "For Riley."

"Let's do it," added Disgust.

"Here we come, Riley," Fear said in the calmest voice Joy had ever heard from him.

Through all the uncertainty of the past few days, there was one thing Joy knew to be true: they would do anything for Riley.

"Let's do this!" Joy shouted. "Three . . . two . . . one!"

The four friends detonated the dynamite together. *BOOM!* Memory spheres surged toward the Emotions like a tidal wave.

There was no escape. But they were ready.

"Jump on!" Joy exclaimed.

As the memories thundered into the canyon, the Emotions leaped into the avalanche. They tried to stay afloat, but the weight and speed of the memory spheres pulled them under. The colorful memories cascaded like a rainbow waterfall over the edge of the Sar-chasm.

Joy plunged into the abyss, clinging to the Sense of Self.

Hold on, Riley, she thought. *We're on our way.*

Meanwhile, the scrimmage continued, but unlike during the start of the game, Riley began to make mistake after mistake. She took a shot only for Bree to block it. She took another one and missed again. As time ticked down, the pressure mounted. It was as if that third goal was just out of Riley's reach.

I'M NOT GOOD ENOUGH, Riley's Sense of Self repeated.

With the puck again, Riley plowed toward the goal. But someone was in her way.

"You have to score!" Anxiety shouted.

Riley shoved the player with her shoulder, causing the person to fall to the ice and slide into the boards. But Riley's sole focus was reaching that goal—

WHACK!

She smashed the puck toward the net, but Bree stopped it again.

"Arrrgghhh!" Anxiety groaned.

Coach blew her whistle. "Andersen!" she shouted. "Penalty box! Two minutes!"

As Riley skated to the penalty box, she noticed the other girls helping Grace off the ice.

"Grace! Are you okay?" Bree called. "She hit you really hard."

Sadness, Ennui, Envy, and Embarrassment gasped.

"We hurt Grace!" Envy exclaimed in horror.

"It all happened so fast!" Anxiety wailed. "I didn't even see her."

Riley skated to the penalty box, breathing hard.

I'M NOT GOOD ENOUGH.

"Oh, no, what did I do?" Anxiety wrung her hands. She frantically began pressing buttons on the console. "No, no. I can fix it. I can fix it."

Joy splashed into the Stream of Consciousness. As she swirled and spun, she lost her grip on the Sense of Self.

She couldn't tell up from down among the tumult of memories that sank into the water around her.

A faint glow caught her eye, and she swam toward it. Relief flooded through her as she realized it was the Sense of Self. The moment she grabbed it, the current pulled her and the memories through the twists and turns of the Sar-chasm.

Just when Joy thought she couldn't hold her breath any longer, the memories burst through a wall, pouring into the Belief System. Joy and the other Emotions flew in with the stream and were pushed to the shore. Joy coughed and sputtered. She couldn't believe her plan had actually worked.

Then she noticed the memory of Riley's hockey penalty moving toward the shore. A belief string sprouted from it and extended toward Headquarters.

"What? No!" Joy exclaimed.

But there was nothing she could do at the moment. They needed to get Riley's Sense of Self up to Headquarters. She would have to figure out what to do with the bad memories and beliefs later.

"Come on!" she shouted to the other Emotions.

They dashed to the elevator, unsure of what they would find in Headquarters.

ADNESS • ANGER • ANXIETY • DISGUST • EMBARRASSMENT • ENNUI • ENVY • FEAR
MBARRASSMENT • ENNUI • ENVY • FEAR • JOY • SADNESS • ANGER • ANXIETY • DISGU
ESS • ANGER • ANXIETY • DISGUST • EMBARRASSMENT • ENNUI • ENVY • FEAR • JOY
MBARRASSMENT • ENNUI • ENVY • FEAR • JOY • SADNESS • ANGER • ANXIETY • DISGU
EAR • JOY • SADNESS • ANGER • ANXIETY • DISGUST • EMBARRASSMENT • ENNUI • E
NVY • FEAR • JOY • SADNESS • ANGER • ANXIETY • DISGUST • EMBARRASSMENT • EN
XIETY • DISGUST • EMBARRASSMENT • ENNUI • ENVY • FEAR • JOY • SADNESS • AN
ENT • ENNUI • ENVY • FEAR • JOY • SADNESS • ANXIETY • DISGUST • EMBARRASSM
Y • DISGUST • EMBARRASSMENT • ENNUI • ENVY • FEAR • JOY • SADNESS • ANGER
NT • ENNUI • ENVY • FEAR • JOY • SADNESS • ANGER • ANXIETY • DISGUST • EMBARR
ANGER • ANXIETY • DISGUST • EMBARRASSMENT • ENNUI • ENVY • FEAR • JOY • SAD
ASSMENT • ENNUI • ENVY • FEAR • JOY • SADNESS • ANXIETY • DISGUST • EMBARRA
ADNESS • ANGER • ANXIETY • DISGUST • EMBARRASSMENT • ENNUI • ENVY • FEAR
MBARRASSMENT • ENNUI • ENVY • FEAR • JOY • SADNESS • ANGER • ANXIETY • DISGU
ESS • ANGER • ANXIETY • DISGUST • EMBARRASSMENT • ENNUI • ENVY • FEAR • JOY
BARRASSMENT • ENNUI • ENVY • FEAR • JOY • SADNESS • ANGER • ANXIETY • DISGU
EAR • JOY • SADNESS • ANGER • ANXIETY • DISGUST • EMBARRASSMENT • ENNUI • AN
NVY • FEAR • JOY • SADNESS • ANGER • ANXIETY • DISGUST • EMBARRASSMENT • EN
XIETY • DISGUST • EMBARRASSMENT • ENNUI • ENVY • FEAR • JOY • SADNESS • ANG
ENT • ENNUI • ENVY • FEAR • JOY • SADNESS • ANXIETY • DISGUST • EMBARRASSM
Y • DISGUST • EMBARRASSMENT • ENNUI • ENVY • FEAR • JOY • SADNESS • ANGER
NT • ENNUI • ENVY • FEAR • JOY • SADNESS • ANGER • ANXIETY • DISGUST • EMBARR
ANGER • ANXIETY • DISGUST • EMBARRASSMENT • ENNUI • ENVY • FEAR • JOY • SAD
ASSMENT • ENNUI • ENVY • FEAR • JOY • SADNESS • ANXIETY • DISGUST • EMBARRAS
ADNESS • ANGER • ANXIETY • DISGUST • EMBARRASSMENT • ENNUI • ENVY • FEAR
MBARRASSMENT • ENNUI • ENVY • FEAR • JOY • SADNESS • ANGER • ANXIETY • DIS
ESS • ANGER • ANXIETY • DISGUST • EMBARRASSMENT • ENNUI • ENVY • FEAR • JO
MBARRASSMENT • ENNUI • ENVY • FEAR • JOY • SADNESS • ANGER • ANXIETY • DISGU
EAR • JOY • SADNESS • ANGER • ANXIETY • DISGUST • EMBARRASSMENT • ENNUI • E
NVY • FEAR • JOY • SADNESS • ANGER • ANXIETY • DISGUST • EMBARRASSMENT • EN
XIETY • DISGUST • EMBARRASSMENT • ENNUI • ENVY • FEAR • JOY • SADNESS • AN
ENT • ENNUI • ENVY • FEAR • JOY • SADNESS • ANXIETY • DISGUST • EMBARRASSM
Y • DISGUST • EMBARRASSMENT • ENNUI • ENVY • FEAR • JOY • SADNESS • ANGER
NT • ENNUI • ENVY • FEAR • JOY • SADNESS • ANGER • ANXIETY • DISGUST • EMBAR
ANGER • ANXIETY • DISGUST • EMBARRASSMENT • ENNUI • ENVY • FEAR • JOY • SAD
ASSMENT • ENNUI • ENVY • FEAR • JOY • SADNESS • ANXIETY • DISGUST • EMBARRAS

Chapter 28

Sitting in the penalty box, Riley had never felt so stressed before. It was as though everything she'd ever worked for in her entire life was coming down to this one game, and she wasn't sure if she could succeed anymore. Why couldn't she play better? Why couldn't she just finish this? She had missed so many shots. She was playing like such a loser. Was she even good enough to make three goals? She'd been so certain earlier, but minute by minute, her chance at proving herself was slipping away. She began to hyperventilate. Her heart raced and her leg trembled.

"Come on, Riley. Get it together," she whispered to herself.

In Headquarters, Anxiety gripped the edges of the console, her knuckles white with tension. "Come on, Riley! Get it together!"

Anxiety began spiraling out of control. She spun around the console, driving hard and pressing buttons and pulling levers. She moved so quickly that she formed a tornado around the console.

"You have to score, Riley!" Anxiety demanded. "Or this will all have been for nothing!"

"Anxiety!" Envy exclaimed. "You're putting too much pressure on her!"

Envy tried to reach the console but was flung backward by the power of Anxiety's spiral. Embarrassment tried next, but he couldn't break through, either.

Riley couldn't catch her breath. She took off her helmet as her penalty time—and the time left in the game—wound down.

The other Emotions watched with horror and helplessness as Anxiety's spiral worsened. Headquarters shook, sending piles of construction material toppling over. Sparks flew off the console as it went into overdrive.

Sadness looked at the Sense of Self. She rushed to it with the other Emotions close behind. To help Riley, they needed to get the Sense of Self off the pedestal. But no matter how much they yanked, pulled, and shoved, it wouldn't budge.

Riley hunched over, struggling to catch her breath.

I can't do it, she thought. *I'm not good enough. I'm not good enough. I'm not good enough.*

"All right, ladies!" Coach said. "Let's take a breather!"

Grace looked at Riley in the penalty box. She knew something was wrong.

At that moment, Joy and the other Emotions emerged from the elevator. They were stunned to see the chaos unfolding in Headquarters.

"Sadness!" Joy called.

"Joy! Help!" Sadness replied. She and the other Emotions were still struggling with the Sense of Self. Joy's group joined the others at the pedestal.

"Come on!" Sadness shouted. "We can do this!"

But even the added strength of Joy, Anger, Disgust, and Fear wasn't enough to remove Anxiety's Sense of Self.

"It's not working!" Disgust exclaimed.

"It's Anxiety!" said Sadness.

Joy looked toward the swirling vortex that surrounded Anxiety and the console. Determined, she handed the old Sense of Self to Sadness.

She pushed against the wind only to be blown backward and nearly lost her balance. She tried again. Step by step and inch by inch, she moved closer to the console until she finally broke through the raging vortex.

Inside, it was silent. Anxiety stood at the console, tense and still.

"Anxiety! Stop!" Joy demanded.

She moved to grab Anxiety, but her arms went straight through her! Seven clones of Anxiety materialized, each standing at the console in a different position. As quickly as she had multiplied, Anxiety combined into a single figure once more.

"Anxiety?" Joy said, confused. But there was no response.

She analyzed the orange Emotion more closely. She could see her twitching and glitching like an image on an old television. Anxiety seemed to be paralyzed, unable to release the controls.

"Anxiety," Joy repeated. "You don't get to choose who Riley is."

Anxiety's hands seemed to grasp the controls even tighter.

"You need to let her go."

After a moment, Anxiety released the controls.

Joy took her chance. She grabbed Anxiety and pulled her out of the vortex. They tumbled to the other side of the room.

Joy scrambled to her feet and rushed to the Sense of Self pedestal. She yanked on the Sense of Self, and this time, it popped off the pedestal. Sadness handed Joy the original Sense of Self, and Joy put it into place.

I'm a good person.

But the storm—and Riley's panic attack—continued to rage.

Joy was confounded. Why hadn't it worked? What was going on?

An exhausted Anxiety called to her. "Joy, I'm sorry. I was just trying to protect her. But you're right. We don't get to choose who Riley is."

Joy looked from Anxiety to the broken Back of the Mind tube to the Sense of Self. She thought about all the bad memories she had banished to the Back of the Mind. She had insisted those memories were hurting Riley and that was the reason they needed to be sent far away. *We keep the best and toss the rest!* she used to say.

Like Anxiety, she had wanted to protect Riley, because she only wanted the best, most positive things for her girl. But in trying to do so, she had made decisions for Riley. She had tried to turn Riley into someone she wasn't.

The Sense of Self pedestal pulsated with light as new

belief strings from the Back of the Mind memories fought to break through. They were being blocked by the original Sense of Self.

Joy knew what she had to do. She walked to the pedestal and ripped out the Sense of Self.

The Emotions gasped.

"Joy! What are you doing?" Disgust cried.

Suddenly, the light from the Belief System burst forth. All of Headquarters glowed, and the entire Mind World illuminated.

The light from Riley's beliefs washed over Joy, warming her heart and calming her mind. She had Riley's strength within her, shared from every single piece that made their girl who she was.

They hadn't lost Riley. They just needed to let her shine.

A new Sense of Self formed on the pedestal. Joy approached it, noticing how it continued to morph and shift, never staying in one state.

I'm selfish.

I'm kind.

I'm not good enough.

I'm a good person.

I need to fit in, but I want to be myself.

I'm brave, but I get scared.

Success is everything.

I make mistakes.

I'm nice.

I'm mean.

I'm a good friend.

I'm a terrible friend.

I'm strong.

I'm weak.

I need help sometimes.

Joy admired the Sense of Self, every form more beautiful than the last. She didn't know who Riley would become, but she would love all of her—always. She wrapped her arms around the Sense of Self.

Sadness joined Joy. She was quickly followed by the rest of the Emotions. Each one hugged the Sense of Self, pouring all their compassion, acceptance, and love into their embrace.

The swirling vortex slowed and dissipated, allowing Riley to catch her breath. It was like she had emerged from the depths of the ocean. She felt the grains of wood from the bench under her hands. She heard the laughter of the other players. She took deep breaths, allowing her racing heart to slow.

She finally noticed Bree and Grace. Their brows were furrowed with concern.

"Riley, are you okay?" asked Grace.

"Yeah. I mean, no," Riley finally admitted.

The whole time at camp, Riley had felt like she hadn't known who she was anymore, like she needed to be a different Riley or a better Riley. Something had nearly snapped in her during that last drive for the goal. She'd almost let the stress get the best of her. Perhaps that was the push she had needed to experience a moment of clarity, seeing beyond the game and the goal and the need to be perfect.

Because the Riley who cared only about being the best and who was willing to power through anyone and anything to achieve it wasn't the Riley she wanted to be. She didn't want or need to be *the* best. She just wanted to be the best Riley. What more could anyone ask of her? What more could she ask of herself? And now it was time to come clean to her best friends.

"I was such a jerk to you guys. When you told me you were going to a different school, I freaked out, and—" She sighed. "I'm so sorry. If you don't wanna be friends anymore, I get it. But I just really hope that you can forgive me. Someday."

Bree and Grace exchanged glances. They smiled and held out their hands to Riley for their signature fist bump.

Riley met their fist bump and then wrapped her two best friends in a big hug.

"Let's go, ladies!" Coach Roberts called.

"Come on," said Grace. "We've got a game to finish."

Grace and Bree skated back to their positions, but Riley continued to stand in the penalty box. She was deep in thought.

In Headquarters, the Emotions watched the screen, relieved that Riley had patched things up with Grace and Bree.

Sadness noticed glowing golden particles pulling from Joy and floating to the console. Eventually, a stream of sparkles led from Joy to the controls.

"Joy," said Sadness, "Riley wants you."

Joy was terrified of disturbing the moment. After everything she had done and all the mistakes she had made, she had wondered if her connection to Riley had been severed completely. But now Riley seemed to be calling to Joy.

The Emotions parted to make a path for Joy. She cautiously walked to the console. When she touched the controls, it emitted a yellow glow.

Riley smiled. She skated onto the ice. A player passed the puck to her. Riley paused for a moment. Instead of charging at the goal before time ran out, she passed the puck to Val. The Fire Hawks called to each other, having fun passing the puck and showing off their skills.

Grace got the puck next. She couldn't help giggling as she joined in the moment of levity after an intense game. She passed the puck to Bree, who passed it to Riley even though they were on different teams. The three best friends had fun on the ice, the way they had wanted to from the start.

Riley looped around, enjoying the feel of the ice under her skates; the smooth, secure motion of her hockey stick strokes; and the crisp, cool scent of the arena she'd grown to love. Joy matched Riley's movements, and they glided and skated together almost as one. Joy had never felt such overwhelming pride and love for her girl.

Chapter 29

The final buzzer went off. The game was over, and Riley hadn't made her third goal. And yet she was still okay. She heard Grace, Bree, Val, and Dani congratulating each other.

She had found the courage to be honest with Bree and Grace, and now it was time to do the same with the Fire Hawks. She approached Val and Dani.

"I'm sorry about how I was playing earlier. I got too caught up in becoming a Fire Hawk. I look up to you guys so much . . . and I want to play on varsity, and I'm terrified to play on varsity, and I want to be with my friends, and I want new friends, and I want for things to never change, but they are and . . . I don't know." She took a shaky breath. "I'm a mess, and everything just looks so easy for everyone else."

"I mess up all the time," Val assured Riley.

"You do?" Riley asked in surprise.

"Yeah, I'm—I'm just really good at hiding it."

"I have no idea what I'm doing ever!" Dani blurted out.

"Oh my gosh, me either!" Grace laughed in relief.

The girls all began talking at once.

"I had no idea you felt that way!"

"I'm totally a mess!"

"It feels so good to say that out loud!"

When Riley had approached her friends, she wasn't sure how the conversation would go. But she never would have anticipated this. Riley's honesty allowed everyone else to admit their own insecurities and weaknesses. She was proud of her friends—and herself.

Bree turned to Riley. "We should have told you sooner about the school thing."

"Sorry, Riley," Grace added. "We didn't know how to tell you, so I just screamed it in your face."

"It's okay," said Riley, feeling lighter than she had all during camp. But there was one last admission to make to the Fire Hawks. Riley took a deep breath. "I'm not from Michigan. I'm from Minnesota."

The Fire Hawks stared at her, and then everyone burst into giggles.

As Riley headed off with her teammates to the locker room, all the Emotions gathered around the new Sense of Self on its pedestal.

The Sense of Self looked different, stretching and morphing into various shapes and fading from one color to the next, like an alien object in constant flux.

Joy gingerly reached out to the new Sense of Self, feeling its warmth on her hand. She knew it would probably continue to change for a while.

Anxiety wrung her hands nervously. "I'm—I'm sorry," she told everyone. "About everything. I didn't mean to cause such a mess."

The Emotions glanced around Headquarters, which looked like one of Pouchy's dynamite bundles had gone off inside—several times.

" 'Mess' is one way to describe it," Disgust said, pulling a face.

"You all must hate me!" Anxiety tugged at her hair.

"There was talk of punting . . ." Anger said under his breath.

"I was just trying to help Riley," Anxiety insisted. "I was just trying—"

"We know." Joy put a hand on Anxiety's shoulder.

"We're all trying to help Riley in our own way. None of us are perfect."

She smiled at the screen. Riley was finally together with Bree and Grace, laughing. They'd even found some funnel cake in the cafeteria.

"Neither is our girl. Because she's not supposed to be. She's just supposed to be Riley."

The Emotions all nodded in agreement, watching as the new Sense of Self stretched into an amorphous bundle.

"Always changing, always growing," Joy whispered. "And we'll be here for her every step of the way."

"Wait, you guys seriously have a half day because of the heat?" Riley propped up her phone on her bed so Bree and Grace could still see her on their three-way video call as she stuffed papers and her school tablet into her backpack. It was several months after camp, and their freshman year of high school was in full swing. The girls had promised one another that they would video chat in the mornings to hold them over until they could meet up in the afternoon. "How is that even possible?" Riley said, searching for her math textbook.

CHAPTER 29

"Dude, have you been outside?" Grace asked. "There's, like, a bizarre heat wave going on."

"Not all high schools in the Bay Area are fancy and have air-conditioning," Bree quipped.

"Only the best ones," Riley said teasingly.

"Hey!" Grace snorted. "At least *our* school has a fall dance! You have whatever that collaborative harvest festival thing is."

"Yeah, it's super weird," Riley agreed. "I don't even know if I'm going to go."

"Aw, you should," Bree said. "It sounds kind of fun."

"And you don't have to worry about finding a date," Grace said, laughing.

Riley smiled to herself, daydreaming for a moment about being at Bree and Grace's high school and taking Lance Slashblade to the fall dance as her date.

"I think the Fire Hawks are going to wear their jerseys to the festival," Riley commented. "Does your school hockey team wear their jerseys to the dance?"

"I'm not sure," Bree said. "Our tryouts aren't until next week."

"Wait—isn't today the day you find out if you made the team?" Grace asked, suddenly remembering.

Riley gulped. It *was* the big day. After camp, Coach

Roberts had encouraged Riley to officially try out for the team. Riley thought it had gone well. There hadn't been any hat trick, but it had been nice that Val, Dani, and the others had all wished her luck beforehand.

"Yeah," Riley said, her voice a little tight with nerves. "Coach is going to email the list out this afternoon."

"I'm sure you made it," Bree said. "I mean, how could you not?"

"Seriously, you crushed it at the skills camp," Grace said. "You crushed it so hard that you literally crushed some of the other players."

"I've apologized for knocking you over like a million times!" Riley protested, though all three friends were smiling. "Will you ever forgive me?"

"Depends how much victory funnel cake you buy me," Grace said.

"When you get the news that you made the team," Bree added, grinning.

Riley laughed, shook her head, and zipped up her backpack. "I've gotta go, or I'm going to be late for school." She paused. "I miss you both."

Bree and Grace waved. "We miss you, too. See you after school?"

"You know it," Riley said.

CHAPTER 29

Anxiety could hardly stand the pressure. She tugged at her turtleneck and chewed on her fingernails as she watched the minutes pass by on Riley's phone, which rested on the table beside their girl.

"Six minutes!" She vibrated nervously. "Six minutes!"

All the Emotions had their eyes fixed on the screen as Riley sat in the cafeteria. She was surrounded by the Fire Hawks. Her (maybe) future teammates had gathered with her to wait for the tryout results.

"Hey, Minnesota"—Val passed Riley a bag of pretzels—"how long are you going to stare at your phone?"

Riley chewed her lip. "Coach said she'd email the list of who made the team by two p.m."

"What happens if we don't become a Fire Hawk?" Anxiety fretted.

"Anxiety," Joy cautioned her gently.

But Anxiety was worked up. "Thanks for asking, Joy. I'll tell you!" She popped up her projection screen and frantically began scrolling.

"First, Mom and Dad are very disappointed." The projection board flashed an image of Riley's parents shaking their heads. "We don't go pro, and we find work as an ethnomusicologist, even though we don't really know what that is, and"—the screen showed Riley standing beside a xylophone and holding a clipboard before that morphed into an image of a gravestone—"we have no friends, and we die alone. *Ahhh!*"

Joy smiled, shook her head, and soothingly placed a hand on the orange Emotion's shoulder. As soon as she did, Anxiety untensed—for the most part.

"Okay, well, none of that is happening right now. Is it, Anxiety?"

"No . . ."

"So why don't we take a seat in our special chair?" Joy suggested, guiding Anxiety to a plushy massage chair.

"Yeah, that's a great idea," Anxiety said.

As Joy turned on the chair, Anxiety sighed. "Oh yeah, that's the stuff."

"We can't control whether Riley makes the team," Joy reminded everyone. "But what can we control?"

"Well, um . . ." Anxiety thought. "Oh! We have a Spanish test tomorrow. We need to study!"

"You're right!" Joy gasped. "We totally—"

"Olvidamos," Anxiety finished for her.

Joy raised an eyebrow. "What's that mean?"

" 'Forgot.' "

"Nice job, Anxiety!" Disgust and Envy said together.

"Thanks for the reminder," Fear and Sadness told her.

"We're learning Spanish?" Ennui asked from the couch.

Anxiety blushed a deeper shade of orange. "Thanks, guys."

"Plus we followed our new varsity-caliber training program," Joy said.

"Oh, I wish I thought of that," Envy whined.

"News flash: you did!" Joy exclaimed.

"Wait, you're right!" Envy replied. "I did! I'm jealous of myself. Thanks for the reminder!"

"You're welcome!" a high-pitched cartoon voice called from somewhere inside Headquarters.

"Who said that?" Joy asked, startled.

"It's my new buddy," Anger told her. He turned around to reveal none other than Pouchy fastened around his waist.

"Hi, everybody!" Pouchy cried.

"Confetti if we make the team!" Anger declared as Pouchy spit out a plume of colorful confetti all over Fear.

"Gah!" Fear yelped.

"That's great," Joy said. "But either way, we love our girl."

"Confetti if we don't!" Anger cheered. Pouchy spit even

more confetti at Fear, causing him to run off with his arms flailing.

Just then, Riley's phone beeped on the cafeteria table. The Emotions gasped.

"Is it Coach's email?" Val asked Riley.

But as Riley picked up her phone, she realized it was something even sweeter: a photo from Grace and Bree with the message "Good luck today!"

"Oh, I miss those girls," Joy said.

"Me too," agreed Disgust.

The school bell chimed, signaling that it was three minutes before class began.

"It's three minutes to two," Anxiety breathed. "You got this, Riley."

Joy nodded. "She's got this . . ."

"Yeah! 'Cause she's got us! Woo! Yeah!" Embarrassment cheered with his fist up. He got shy as everyone turned to look at him. "Right? Maybe?"

"All right, Embarrassment!" Joy exclaimed. "Everybody, look at Embarrassment!" She gave him a high five.

Sadness patted Embarrassment on the arm. "Nice job, big guy."

In the cafeteria, Riley began gathering her phone and

books. Coach's email still hadn't come through, but she needed to get to her next class.

Val must have understood how much making the team meant to Riley, because before she left, she offered her a fist bump. "If you don't make it this year, there's always next year."

Riley smiled. "I know."

And all the Emotions swelled with pride.

"I love our girl," Anxiety sighed.

"How could you not?" Joy agreed. She gazed at the shimmering, shifting Sense of Self and thought back on all the perfectly imperfect moments that had made Riley who she was right then.

In front of her locker mirror, Riley put up her hair in a scraggly bun and blew a strand out of her face just as her phone beeped with a new email. She looked down at it and read the message, and a small smile spread across her lips.

Joy nodded proudly. No matter what happened now or in the future, Joy and the Emotions loved *all* of their girl—every messy, beautiful piece of her.

SADNESS • ANGER • ANXIETY • DISGUST • EMBARRASSMENT • ENNUI • ENVY • FEAR • JOY